John George Hodgins

The Law and Official Regulations Relating to Public School

Trustees in Rural Settings

and to public school teachers - including decisions of the superior courts

thereon.

John George Hodgins

The Law and Official Regulations Relating to Public School Trustees in Rural Settings
and to public school teachers - including decisions of the superior courts thereon.

ISBN/EAN: 9783337377625

Printed in Europe, USA, Canada, Australia, Japan

Cover: Foto ©Andreas Hilbeck / pixelio.de

More available books at **www.hansebooks.com**

SCHOOL LAW LECTURES—PART I.

NEW AND REVISED EDITION.

————————

THE

LAW AND OFFICIAL REGULATIONS

RELATING TO

PUBLIC SCHOOL TRUSTEES

IN

RURAL SECTIONS,

AND TO

PUBLIC SCHOOL TEACHERS

(INCLUDING DECISIONS OF THE SUPERIOR COURTS THEREON)

AS PRESCRIBED FOR

SECOND AND THIRD CLASS

PROVINCIAL AND COUNTY CERTIFICATES

OF QUALIFICATION.

————————

BEING THE SUBSTANCE OF LECTURES TO NORMAL SCHOOL STUDENTS

BY

J. GEORGE HODGINS, LL.D., *Barrister-at-Law,*

Deputy Minister of Education for Ontario.

————————

TORONTO:

COPP, CLARK & CO., 47 FRONT STREET.

1878.

CONTENTS.

PUBLIC SCHOOL LAW

RELATING TO

TRUSTEES IN RURAL SECTIONS.

PRELIMINARY REMARKS IN REGARD TO THE OFFICE OF TRUSTEE.

NOTE.—There are certain equitable principles which apply to the trustees and their office, (some of which do not arise under the School Law,) to which it is proper to refer in this place, as follows :—

1.—A Trustee defined.

A trustee may be regarded as a person to whom money, or other property or valuables, is intrusted to expend or manage, under certain rules or directions, for the use or benefit of another party.

2.—What a Trustee is expected to do.

In the discharge of his duties, a trustee is required to use the customary care and diligence usually exercised by a man of ordinary prudence and vigilance in the management of his own affairs.

3.—Responsibilities of a Trustee.

A trustee is responsible :—

(a) For his own acts, and for the acts of his colleagues done with his knowledge.

(b) For all breaches of trust or default committed by himself, or by his colleagues, to which he is privy, or in which he expressly or tacitly acquiesces, or which would not have happened but for his own negligence, act or default.

(c) (*Under the School Law*) a trustee is personally responsible for neglect of duty, refusal to act when lawfully required to do so, or for loss of school money through his wilful act, negligence or carelessness in not keeping the school open, in not reporting to Inspector, and in not compelling the attendance of absentees.

4.—What a Trustee may do.

He may, with the consent of his colleagues :

(*a*) Defray out of the trust fund expenses legitimately and properly incurred. (See *Decisions of the Courts*, chap. iii, sec. 12, *No.* (10).

(*b* —*Under the School Law*)—Receive remuneration as collector of school rates.

(*c* —*Under the School Law*)—Receive payment for a school site.

5.—What a Trustee may not do.

Unless modified by Statute, or other authoritative direction, a trustee cannot lawfully :

(*a*) Receive, even with the consent of his colleagues, any salary or remuneration for his services in the capacity of trustee.

(*b*) Make any personal profit out of the trust.

(*c*) Mix up trust money or accounts with his own private money or accounts.

(*d* —*Under the School Law*)—Enter into a contract with, or have a pecuniary claim (except in the two instances mentioned above) on the corporation of which he is a member.

(*e* —*Ibid*.)—Act as bookseller's agent, or sell books, maps, apparatus or other requisites to the school. (See sec. 9 of chap. xiii.)

CHAPTER I.

THE OFFICE OF TRUSTEE.

Section 1.—Who may be a Public School Trustee.

Any assessed freeholder, householder or tenant, resident in a public school section, may be elected a trustee of such section.

2.—Who may not be a Public School Trustee.

The law excludes the following persons from the office of school trustee :—

(*a*) A non-resident of the section, or school division. (School Act, see secs. 18, 48 and 91.)

(*b*) A resident, who is not an assessed ratepayer.— (*Ibid*.

(*c*) An inspector of public schools.— Sec. 226.

(*d*) A teacher in a high or public school.—*Ibid*.

3.—The Office of School Trustee may be vacated as follows :

(*a*) *By refusal to act*, and payment of *five* dollars as a penalty for such refusal, immediately after election to office. (*Ibid*, sec. 236.)

(*b*) *By resignation*, with the consent in writing of his colleagues, and of the inspector of public schools. (*Ibid.* sec. 20.)

(*c*) *Neglect to make Verbal Declaration.*—On being fined five dollars by a magistrate for neglect, or refusal, to make a verbal declaration of office before the chairman of the school meeting, within two weeks after election as trustee. (*Ibid.* sec. 247.)

NOTE.—The declaration of office, if made at any time previously to being summoned before a magistrate, may be held to rebut the "evidence of his refusing to serve" as trustee (For powers of trustee-elect, before being fined for not making the declaration of office, see chapter vi. on "*Public School Meetings.*")

(*d*) *Neglect of Duty.*—On being fined *twenty* dollars for neglecting or refusing to perform the duties of his office—not having, on his election (as in (*a*) above), refused to accept office, and having paid the prescribed penalty of *five* dollars for such refusal. (*Ibid.* sec. 236.)

(*e*) *Removal.*—By actual removal of domicile from the section.

(*f*) *Non-Residence.*—By three consecutive months' absence from the meetings of the school corporation without being authorized by resolution entered upon the trustees' minute book. (*Ibid.* sec. 88.)

(*g*) *Outside the Boundaries.*—On being placed outside of the section boundaries, by reason of an alteration in them. (See note to section 6 of this chapter.)

(*h*) *Conviction* of any felony or misdemeanor.

4.—Verbal Declaration of Office required to be made.

Within two weeks after his election, the new trustee is required to make the following verbal declaration of office, in presence of the chairman of the school meeting :—

" I will truly and faithfully, to the best of my judgment and ability, " discharge the duties of the office of school trustee, to which I have " been elected." (School Act, secs. 19 and 247.)

NOTE.—If the chairman himself be elected trustee, he is required to make the foregoing declaration of office in presence of the secretary of the school meeting. In the case of neglect or refusal to do so—in either case—the trustee-elect subjects himself to a fine of *twenty* dollars, to be recovered before a magistrate, for the benefit of the section. Immediately on the imposition of this fine, the office is vacated, and a new election should be held; but, in the meantime, the *bona fide* acts (of the trustee who was fined, if he should perform any), are binding upon the section. (See note to (*c*) of section 3, and note to section 6 of this chapter.)

5.—Trustee's Three Years' Term of Office.

Every trustee holds office for three years, and until his successor is elected. This rule does not apply to the second and third trustees elected at a *first* school meeting in a section. One of these trustees (the second elected) holds office for two years, and the other (the third elected) holds it for one year, and in all cases until their respective successors are appointed. (*Ibid*, sec. 17.)

NOTE.—After serving his full term, a person cannot be compelled to act again as trustee until after the expiration of four years; but he may, with his own consent, be re-elected on his going out of office. This privilege does not extend to a person who declines to act as trustee, and pays the fine of *five* dollars for non-service. Such a person may be elected to fill the next succeeding vacancy, but may again decline to serve, on payment of *five* dollars, as before. (*Ibid*, secs. 36 & 236.)

6.—Who are the Trustees of altered School Sections.

That part of a divided or altered section, in which the school house of the section continues to be situated, is held to be the old or original section. The trustees who live in this old part remain the lawful trustees of the section, and only go out of office on the expiration of their term of service. Those only who, by the alteration of the section, are placed outside of the new boundaries— and thus become non-residents—cease to be trustees when the alteration takes effect (25th of December.) (See (*y*) of sec. 3 above, also "Note" below.)

NOTE.—As a general rule, it is scarcely worth while to anticipate the annual meeting, and elect a trustee or trustees in place of the one (or two) who may cease to hold office on the 25th December, by reason of non-residence, caused by being placed outside the new boundaries, as explained above. The remaining trustee or trustees in the section (as well as the secretary or inspector) can give notice of the annual school meeting. Should, however, an election be held before the annual meeting, another election must be held on the second Wednesday in January, to fill up the usual vacancy caused by the retiring trustee.

7.—Liability of the original section for old debts.

The Court of Common Pleas has decided that one or more alterations in the boundaries of a school section, or the change of ownership of land in the section by many of the ratepayers originally liable, did not relieve the trustees of the responsibility of paying a just debt due by the original section before any such alteration was made. (See decision (4), sec. 13, of chap. ii, p. 21.) This general principle was also incorporated in the Consolidated School Law of 1874, so far as loans made to the trustees of any section is concerned. The land in such section at the time when the loan is effected continues liable for the debt until repaid, even should it in the meantime be placed outside of the boundaries of the school section, by reason of their alteration.

8.—Power of the Retiring Trustee at the Close of his Term.

The restriction on the power of the "retiring trustee," at the close of his term of office, having been removed by the Consolidated School Act, he has now equal power and authority with either of his colleagues to perform all lawful acts up to the day of his leaving office.

9.—Personal Liability of Trustees—How it arises.

The personal responsibility of trustees arises in various ways, (under the School Act and Regulations), among others, as follows :

(a) For neglect to keep open a school during the whole school year, to send in reports to the inspector, or to compel the attendance of absentees under the compulsory clauses of the statute, and the consequent loss of any part of the school fund to the section. (See (j) of this sec., and note to sec. 3, chap. viii.)

(b) For any loss incurred, in consequence of neglect to take security from their secretary-treasurer, collector, or other person entrusted with school moneys. (School Act, sec. 229.)

NOTE.—This security should be lodged with the township council, as required by law.

(c) Neglect to transact trustee business, at trustee meetings duly called (of which each trustee must have due notice). (Ibid. sec. 96.)

NOTE.—Trustees are, of course, free to converse at pleasure with each other, and informally to agree on any school business; but the law declares that—

"The resolution, action, or proceeding of at least two of the trustees is necessary, in order to lawfully bind the school corporation." (Ibid. sec. 99.)

Thus, if a verbal contract or agreement, without the knowledge of the other trustee, be made by two trustees with other parties acting in good faith, such agreement or understanding would necessarily bind the corporation, and not the individual trustees who entered into it, and it can be enforced against the corporation. Thus a contract signed by two trustees, and sealed with the corporate seal, can be enforced against the corporation. This rule also applies to minor purchases and unimportant orders for work required to be done for the corporation, and involving an outlay. (See Fetterly v. Russell & Cambridge (on simple contract debts), 14 Q. B. R. 433.) In such cases trustees should authorize one of themselves, or their secretary, to attend to such matters on their behalf. No trustee (as we have shown) can enter into a contract with the corporation of which he is a member, or have any pecuniary claim on it, except for a school site, or as collector of school rates, when duly appointed by his colleagues. No act of the school corporation requires the assent, or necessarily the presence, of each individual trustee. It is sufficient that each of the three trustees have been individually notified of the trustee meeting, and that a majority of the three trustees thus notified concur in the act itself. The following decisions of the Superior Courts sustain this view:—

(1.) *Two School Trustees can enter into a Contract against the wishes of a third.*—The Court of Common Pleas has decided that a contract entered into by two trustees under the School Acts, with the corporate seal attached, is sufficient; and a plea that it was signed by the two subscribing trustees without the consent or approbation of the third, was *held* to be bad.—*Forbes* v. *Trustees No. 8, Plympton.* 8 C. P. R. 74.

(2.) *But two Trustees cannot act without consulting a third.*—The Court of Queen's Bench has decided that two of the trustees of a school are not competent to act in all cases without consulting a third, and giving him an opportunity of uniting in or opposing the acts of his colleagues.—*Orr* v. *Ranney et al., No. 15, Westminster.* 12 Q. B. R. 377.

(See other decisions of the courts, in section 13, chapter ii. page 21.)

(d) For *wilful neglect* or refusal "to exercise all the corporate "powers vested in them * * * for the fulfilment of any contract or "agreement made by them." (School Act, sec. 238. See also decisions in sec. 10 of this chap., and note to sec. 3 (*b*) of chap. viii.)

(*e*) *Declaration of Office—Duty.*—For refusal or neglect to make the declaration of office, or to perform their lawful duties after having accepted office, a fine of *five* or *twenty* dollars (as the case may be) may be enforced by a magistrate. (See School Act, secs. 237 and 247, sec. 4 of this chapter, page 11.)

(*f*) *Notes of Hand.*—For all notes of hand which they may sign (not authorized by law).

NOTE.—The signature of two or more trustees to notes of hand, and even the affixing to them of the corporate seal, do not necessarily relieve individual trustees of personal responsibility in regard to them, or give to such notes a corporate character, unless they are given for loans raised with which to pay the teacher's salary. In that case they may be given, bearing not more than eight per cent. The law, however, gives trustees ample powers at all times to procure by rate, imposed by themselves, or by the township council, such money as they may require. Trustees who require to borrow money for the purchase of a site and the erection of a school house, can do so by permission of the municipal council; and the council is alone authorized to provide for the repayment of such borrowed money. An exception to this general rule is contained in the 361st section of the Municipal Institutions Act of 1877. This section authorizes "any municipal corporation having surplus moneys set apart for educational purposes, by by-law, to invest the same in a loan or loans to any board or boards of school trustees within the limits of the municipality, for such term or terms, and at such rate or rates of interest as may be agreed upon by and between the parties to such loan or loans respectively, and set forth in such by-law, or may by by-law grant any portion of such moneys or other general funds by way of gift to aid poor school sections within the municipality." (See decision (1) of the Courts, section 3, chapter ii. page 16.)

(*g*) *Unqualified Teachers.*—For the salary of teachers, or assistants (employed by them), who do not possess legal certificates of qualification during the whole period of their engagement. (See chapter ix.)

(*h*) *Refusal to account.*—For their own refusal, or that of their secretary (on their behalf), to furnish either of the school section auditors with the papers or information in their possession, or within their jurisdiction, relative to their school accounts. (See chapter v.)

(*i*) *Account for Moneys.*—For neglect, or refusal, to account to competent authority for school moneys or other school property entrusted to them, or in their possession. (See chapter v.)

(*j*) *Neglect of Law and Regulations.*—For loss to the section, of any portion of the legislative grant (or county assessment), in consequence of their neglect or refusal to keep their school open during the entire year, or of their neglect to make reports and returns to the inspector, or of their refusal to conduct their school according to law or to the official regulations (which have the force of law.)

(k) Further Monetary Penalties for Neglect of Duty :—

(1.) *Twenty* dollars for making a false return to the Inspector.

(2.) *Five* dollars for very week of delay in forwarding their annual report to the Inspector.

(3.) *Five* dollars for neglect in not calling annual or other necessary school meetings.

10.—Legal Decisions on the Personal Liability of Trustees.

(I.) *Personal Liability or neglect or refusal to exercise their Corporate powers.*—The Court of Queen's Bench has decided as follows, in a case where a mandamus *nisi* having been issued to school trustees to levy the amount of a judgment obtained against them, no return was made, and a rule *nisi* for an attachment issued. In answer to this rule, one trustee swore that he always had been and still was desirous to obey the writ, and had repeatedly asked the others to join with him in levying the rate, but that they had refused. Another swore that owing to ill-health, with the consent of his co-trustees and the local superintendent, he had resigned his office before the writ was granted. The court, under these circumstances, discharged the rule *nisi* as against these two, on payment of costs of the application, and granted an attachment against the other trustee, who had taken no notice either of the mandamus or rule.—*Regina* v. *Trustees of School Section No. 27, Tyendinaga.* 20 Q. B. R. 528.

(2.) The Court of Queen's Bench has decided, that, as by the [*twentieth*] clause of the [*twenty-seventh*] section of the Consolidated School Act, the trustees can only be personally liable when they have wilfully neglected or refused to exercise their corporate powers; such neglect or refusal should have been alleged and shown in the award, to warrant its directious to levy on the trustees personally.—*Kennedy* v. *Burness & al, No. 5, Oneida.* 15 Q. B. R. 473.

(3.) *Neglect of Trustees to exercise their Corporate Powers must be proved.*—The Court of Common Pleas also decided another similar case as follows:—In an action of replevin for goods of school trustees distrained under an award for the salary of a school teacher, declaring the trustees individually liable on the ground "that the trustees did not exercise all the corporate powers vested in them by the School Acts for the due fulfilment of the contract" made by them with such teacher. *Held,* that the award as evidence, did not support pleas which averred as required by the [*twentieth*] clause of the [*twenty-seventh*] section of the Consolidated School Act, a wilful neglect or refusal by the trustees to exercise their corporate powers as the ground for making them personally liable. 2. That on the facts, the defendants as trustees were not personally liable, the award ascertaining for the first time the exact amount due to the teacher, and declaring the trustees personally liable without giving them any opportunity to exercise their corporate powers to raise the money to pay it.—*Kennedy* v. *Hull et al, No. 5, Oneida.* 7 C. P. R. 218.

Note.—An award for a teacher's salary cannot now be made. All salary disputes between trustees and teachers must be settled in the Division Courts. (School Act, sec. 105.)

(4.) The same Court has decided that where trustees become personally liable under the statute, it is necessary to show that there has been some adjudication of the fact of wilful neglect or refusal to exercise the corporate powers vested in them for the fulfilment of any contract or agreement made by them, before such liability can be enforced.—*Ranney* v. *Maclem et al,* 9 C. P. R. 192.

(5.) *When Personal Liability of Trustee arises.*—The Court of Queen's Bench has decided that trustees cannot be held liable unless they wilfully neglect to do their duty; not where they decline in good faith to exercise their corporate powers on account of any doubt or legal difficulty which they suppose to exist.—*Vanburen* v. *Bull et al, No. 2, Rawdon.* 19 Q. B. R. 633.

Note.—See also *Tp. Toronto* v. *McBride's,* No. (2) of sec. 15, chap. xlii.

CHAPTER II.

POWERS AND DUTIES OF TRUSTEES.

I.—GENERAL CORPORATE POWERS.

1.—Rural School Trustees to be a Corporation.

The law declares that " the trustees in every school section shall be a corporation, under the name of *The Public School Trustees of Section No.—, in the Township of———, in the County of———.* And no such corporation shall cease by reason of want of trustees. In case of such want (a) any two assessed freeholders or household. ers of the section, or the Inspector, may, by giving *six* days' notice, * * * call a meeting of the assessed freeholders, householders or tenants who shall proceed to elect three trustees. * * * The trustees thus elected shall hold and retire from office, in the manner prescribed " in this Act." (School Act, sec. 21.)

2.—General Powers and Liabilities of a Corporation.

The Consolidated General Interpretation Act further declares that " Words making any association or number of persons a corporation, or body politic and corporate, shall vest in such corporation power to sue and be sued ; to contract and be contracted with in their corporate name ; to have a common seal,* and to alter or change the same at their pleasure; to have perpetual succession, and power to acquire and hold personal property and movables for the purposes for which the corporation is constituted, and to alienate the same at pleasure ; and shall also vest in any majority of the members of the corporation, the power to bind the others by their acts ; and shall exempt the individual members of the corporation from personal liability for its debts or obligations or acts, provided they do not contravene the provisions of the Act incorporating them. (Rev. Stat. c. i, s. 8, cl. 24.) But no corporation shall carry on the business of banking [*i. e.* taking or issuing promissory notes, &c.,] unless when such power is expressly conferred on them by Statute. (See " *Decisions of Courts*," next section (1).

3.—Legal Decisions regarding School Trustee Corporations.

(1.) *Circulation of School Orders on Treasurer, an Act of Banking contrary to Law.*—Chief Justice Draper thus condemns unauthorized acts of banking on the part of corporations. He says : " The evidence given at this trial shows that a practice had grown up for the defendants to give orders on their treasurer, which,

---

* A corporation being an invisible body, cannot manifest its will by oral communication ; a peculiar mode has therefore been devised for the authentic expression of its intention,—namely, the affixing of its common seal ; and it is held that though the particular members may express their private consent by words or signing their names, yet this does not bind the corporation ; it is the fixing of the seal, and that only, which unites the several assents of the individuals composing it, and makes one joint assent of the whole.—*Smith's Mercantile Law, b. i, chap. 4.*

when he had accepted them, got into circulation, and at last found their way into the collector's hands in payment of taxes. Such a practice seems to me at variance with the spirit, if not the intention, of the Consolidated Municipal Act, which enacts that no council shall act as a banker, or issue any bond, bill, note, debenture, or other undertaking of any kind, or in any form of the nature of a bank-bill or note, or intended to form a circulating medium, or to pass as money ; and any bond, bill, note, debenture, or other undertaking issued in contravention of this section, shall be void.—*In re Munson* v. *The Municipality of Collingwood*, 9 C. P. R. 497.

(2.) *A Corporation aggregate is not bound to appear as Witnesses in Court, but its Individual Members may be supœnaed.*—The Court of Common Pleas has decided that a corporation aggregate is not bound to appear at the trial as witnesses, under a notice served on its attorney under the Consolidated ,Statute 22 Vict. chap. 32, sec. 15. If the individual members are required to appear, they must be individually subpœnaed.—*Trustees No. 2, Dunwich* v. *McBeath*, 4 C. P. R. 228.

(3.) *Two School Trustees can enter into a Contract against the wishes of a third.*— The Court of Common Pleas has decided that a contract entered into by two trustees under the School Acts, with the corporate seal attached, is sufficient, and a plea that it is signed by the two subscribing trustees without the consent or approbation of the third, [but not without his knowledge,] was *held* to be bad.— *Forbes* v. *Trustees, No. 8, Plympton.* 8 C. P. R. 74. (See next decision.)

(4.) *But two Trustees cannot Act without consulting a third.*—The Court of Queen's Bench has decided that two of the trustees of a school are not competent to act in all cases without consulting the third, and giving him an opportunity of uniting in or opposing the acts of his colleagues.—*Orr* v. *Ranney et al, No. 15, Westminster.* 12 Q. B. R. 377.

(5.) *A Trustee, when sued for a Corporate Act, entitled to Notice of Action.*—The Court of Common Pleas has decided, in a case of alleged trespass under a warrant, that a school trustee who is sued for any act done in his corporate capacity, is entitled to notice of action, and that the action must be brought within six months; and that a school trustee, acting in the discharge of his duty as such, in entitled to the protection of, and comes within the Consolidated Statute, 22 Vict., chap. 126, notwithstanding he should have signed a warrant individually, instead of in his corporate capacity.—*Spry* v. *Munby et al, No. 15 Rawdon.* 11 C. P. R. 285.

(6.) *Protection of Trustees, Collectors, and other lawful School Officers.*—The following are the provisions of the Act for the protection of magistrates and others, to which the judge in the foregoing decisions referred.

Sec. 1. Every action brought against any Justice of the Peace, for any act done by him in the execution of his duty as such Justice, with respect to any matter within his jurisdiction as said Justice, *or against any other officer or person fulfilling any public duty, for anything by him done in the performance of such public duty,* [interpreted by the court in the foregoing case (11 C. P. R. 285) to apply to school trustees and to collectors of school rates, when acting under the trustees' lawful warrant,] whether any of such duties arise out of the common law or be imposed by Act of Parliament, either Imperial or Provincial, shall be an action on the case for a tort, and in the declaration it shall be expressly alleged that such act was done maliciously and without reasonable and probable cause ; and if at the trial of any such action, upon the general issue pleaded, the plaintiff fails to prove such allegation, he shall be nonsuited, or a verdict shall be given for defendant.   •   •   •   •   •   •

Sec. 20. So far as applicable, the whole of this Act shall apply for the protection of every officer and person mentioned in the first section hereof, for anything done in the execution of his office, as therein expressed.

NOTE.—The one hundred and sixty seventh section of the Consolidated Public School Act of 1874, also provides that "Trustees shall not be liable to any prosecution, or the payment of any damages for acting under any by-law of a municipal council before it has been quashed."

II.—Powers and Duties of Trustees in Regard to the Site and School House.

4.—Duty of Trustees in regard to the Site of a School House.

A change of site can only take place by consent of a majority of the ratepayers present at a meeting called by the trustees (or the county inspector). Should a difference of opinion arise at the meeting between a majority of the trustees and the ratepayers on the choice of a new site, the matter must be referred to arbitration, as explained in the chapters relating to "School Meetings" and "School Sites;" but the trustees alone have the legal right to decide upon the size or enlargement of a school site, as provided in sec. 10 of chap. vii.

5.—Trustees to hold School Property by any Title.

Trustees are required by law "To take possession and have the custody and safe keeping of all public school property which has been acquired or given for public school purposes in such section; to acquire and hold as a corporation, by any title whatsoever, any land, movable property, moneys, or income given or acquired at any time for public school purposes, and to hold or apply the same according to the terms on which the same were acquired or received." (School Act, sec. 102, cl. 6. See also sec. 8 of this chapter.)

6.—Necessity for a proper Title to the School Site.

The provision of the law, and especially the one mentioned in section 8, below, which vests all school property in the trustee corporation for the purposes of sale, requires that trustees should, without delay, whenever practicable, obtain a deed,* a bond for a deed, a lease, or other legal instrument, granting to them quiet possession of the school site of their section, in case they have not a sufficient title to it.

(1.) Objection is frequently made to the right of trustees to assess the section for the building of, or repairs to, the school house, where no full legal title to the school premises is vested in them. To remove this objection (although it is only a technical one), trustees should obtain the legal instrument referred to, and have it registered without delay.

(2.) Every public school house and site are exempt from taxation, as provided in the Assessment Act. (Sec. 6, cl. 5.)

7.—Registration of Trustees' Title to School Premises.

The trustees should not fail to register the title to their school site. In case the owner of a site refuses to sell it to them, and the trustees are compelled to take possession of it under an award of arbitrators, they should, on the affidavit of one of their number, verifying the

---

* Form of Deed for the site of the School House, Teacher's Residence, &c., can be obtained free of postage from Messrs. Copp, Clark & Co., Toronto, for 20 cents.

same, register the award in the Registry Office, if the owner should refuse to give them a title under the award.

NOTE.—Want of registration of title does not deprive the trustees of the right to assess and collect money for any of the school purposes of the section.

8.—When Trustees may sell a School Site or other Property.

School trustee corporations can dispose, by sale or otherwise, of any school site or school property which may not be required by them, in consequence of a change of school site; they should convey the same under their corporate seal. The proceeds of the sale are to be applied to lawful school purposes. All sites and other property, given or acquired for public school purposes, vests, therefore, absolutely in the trustee corporation for this purpose. (See "*School Sites,*" chap. vii.)

9.—What constitutes adequate School Accommodation.

The law makes it the duty of trustees to provide adequate accommodation for "at least two-thirds of the children who have the right to attend school, according to the census taken by the trustees for the next preceding year." And now that the "compulsory" law is in force, this duty must be faithfully performed. (See sec. 2 of chap. viii. of these Lectures.) The "accommodation" to be adequate, should include:

(1. *Size of Site.*)—A site of the size mentioned in the regulations in chapter xvii. at the end.

(2. *Size of Rooms.*)—The school house must be of the dimensions fixed by regulation. (See chapter xvii. at the end.) The area in each room shall be at least one hundred and twenty cubic feet of air for each child.* The rooms must also be sufficiently warmed and ventilated, and the premises properly drained.

(3. *Fence.*)—A sufficient fence or paling round the school premises.

NOTE.—The *Ontario Line Fences Act* of 1874 (37 Vic. ch. 25), which applies to school fences, enacts that "Owners of occupied adjoining lands shall make, keep up and repair a just proportion of the fence which marks the boundary between them; or, if there is no fence, they shall so make, keep up and repair the same proportion which is to mark such boundary; and owners of unoccupied, which adjoin occupied, lands, shall, upon their being occupied, be liable to the duty of keeping up and repairing such proportion, and in that respect shall be in the same position as if their land had been occupied at the time of the original fencing, and shall be liable to the compulsory proceedings hereinafter mentioned." (Sec. 1.) The Act further provides (in case of dispute) for the appointment of fence viewers to make an award, which may be enforced as pointed out in the Statute.

(4. *A Play Ground,*) or other satisfactory provision of sufficient extent for physical exercise, within the fences, and off the road.

---

* Thus, for instance, a room for fifty children would require space for 6,000 cubic feet of air. This would be equal to a cube of the following dimensions in feet, viz.: 30 x 20 x 10, which is equivalent to a room 30 feet long by 20 feet wide and 10 feet high.

(5. *A Well*,) or other means of procuring water for the school.

(6. *Separate Offices.*)—Proper and separate offices for both sexes, at some little distance from the school house, from each other, and enclosed with a high and secure fence.

(7. *Furniture, Maps and Apparatus.*)—Suitable school furniture and apparatus, desks, seats, blackboards, maps, presses, and books, &c., necessary for the efficient conduct of the school. (See sec. 14, ch. ii.)

NOTE.—*General Suggestions to Trustees in regard to School House Lots.*—The school ground should, in the rural sections, embrace an acre in extent, and not less than half-an-acre, so as to allow the school house to be set well back from the road, and to furnish play-grounds within the fences. A convenient form for school grounds will be found to be an area of ten rods front by sixteen rods deep, with the school house set back four or six rods from the road. The grounds should be strongly fenced; the yards and outhouses in the rear of the school house should be separated by a high and tight board fence; the front grounds should also be planted with shade trees; shrubs and flowers in their season. Various simple plants, required for illustration in the lessons on botany, might be cultivated near the school house. Flowers, beautiful in themselves, have a most delightful and humanizing influence on children and youth, who should be taught to care for and preserve them from harm on the school premises.

10.—Erection of School House, Teacher's Residence, &o.

The trustees alone have the right to decide upon the cost, size and description of the school house, or teacher's residence, which they shall erect. No ratepayer, public meeting, or committee has any authority to interfere with or control them in this matter. They have also full power to decide what fences, outbuildings, sheds and other accommodations shall be provided, as explained in section 9 of this chapter. To them also exclusively belongs the right to have the school grounds planted with shade trees, and properly laid out.

11.—Restriction on the Use of the School House.

No school house or lot (unless so provided for in an old deed), or any building, furniture, or other thing pertaining thereto, shall be used or occupied for any other purpose than for the use and accommodation of the public school of the section or division, without the express permission of the trustee corporation, and then only after school hours, and on condition that all damages be made good, and cleaning, sweeping, &c., promptly done, or compensation made therefor.

NOTE.—Should trustees abuse this discretion in regard to the use of the school house, they may be restrained by injunction from the Court of Chancery.

12.—Duty in Regard to the Care and Repair of School House.

Trustees should for convenience, appoint one of their number, (or the Secretary-Treasurer or other responsible person,) and give him authority, as well as make it his duty, to keep the school house in

good repair. He should also see to it that the windows are properl
filled with glass; that at a proper season the stove and pipe are in a fi
condition, and suitable wood provided; that the desks and seats are
in good repair; that the outhouses are properly provided with doors
and are frequently cleaned; that the blackboards are painted, the
water supply abundant, and everything provided necessary for the
comfort of the pupils and the efficiency of the school.

13.—Legal Decisions in regard to the School House.

(1.) *Trustees can levy a rate for the erection of a School House.*—The Court of
Queen's Bench has decided that, under the School Act, school trustees are autho-
rized to levy a rate for the erection of a school house in their section.—*Chief
Superintendent of Education, appellant, in re Kelly v. Hedges, Burford, and 13
Windham.* 12 Q. B. R. 531.

(2.) *School House Contracts not valid without trustee Corporate Seal.*—The Court
of Common Pleas has decided that the trustees of a School Section, being a corporation under the School Acts, are not liable as such to pay for a school-house
erected for and accepted by them, not having contracted under seal for the erection
of the same. The seal is required as authenticating the concurrence of the whole
body corporate.—*Marshall v. Trustees, No. 11 Kitley.* 4 C. P. R. 373.

NOTE.—Such a contract, not being binding on the corporation, would be binding on the individual trustees who made it with a third party, acting in good faith. *Query*, whether the trustee-
corporation would not, by subsequently taking possession of the school house, or by some other
act, recognize the validity of the contract?

(3.) *Contract under Seal, signed by a majority of the Corporation, binding.*—The
same Court has also decided the following case:—A contract was entered into by
two of the trustees of a section under their corporate seal for building a school
house; after the house was built the trustees refused to pay, on the plea that the
contract was not legal. A jury having given a verdict in favour of the trustees, a
new trial was ordered, and the former verdict in favour of the trustees was set aside.
The Court *held*, that a contract entered into by *two* trustees under the School Act,
with the corporate seal attached, is sufficient; and a plea that the contract was
signed by the *two* subscribing trustees, with the consent or approbation of the
third, was *held* bad.—*Forbes v. Trustees, No. 8, Plympton.* 8 C. P. R. 73, 74.

(4.) *Alteration of Boundaries no valid ground for refusing to levy rates to pay for
a School House.*—The same court has decided the following case:—The plaintiff recovered a judgment in March, 1858, against the school trustees for a debt due to him
for building a school house for the section, and made several unsuccessful attempts
to obtain payment of the same from the trustees and their successors in office.
The trustees always refused to levy a rate, or to pay the judgment. To an application for a *mandamus* to compel the trustees to levy a rate for payment of the
judgment, the Court *held* that it was no answer that, since the recovery of the
judgment, two alterations had been made in the limits of the section, and that
many changes had taken place among the rate-payers originally liable ; or that
the merits of the claim on which the judgment was founded were capable of being
impeached.—*Johnston v. School Trustees of Harwich*, 20 Q. B. 264, distinguished.
Scott v. Trustees, No. 1 Burgess, and 2 Bathurst. 21 C. P. R. 398.

(5.) *School House and Site in use not liable to be sold on judgment against Trustee
Corporation.*—The Court of Queen's Bench has given judgment as follows :— In a
case in which a school site had been given to the trustees for the purposes of a
school (with the condition that it should revert to the giver in case it should cease
to be used for school purposes), and on which they had erected a school house,
judgment was obtained against the corporation for the money due on the building
contract. The school house and site were actually sold and deeded by the Sheriff;

but the Court held, that the house and land could not lawfully be sold—it being contrary to public policy that a school house in daily use (any more than a court house or gaol) should be held liable upon a writ of execution, as, not the trustees but, the inhabitants of the section are the *cestuis que trust* (*i.e.* the persons for whose benefit the trust was held). The plaintiff should have resorted to his other remedies against the trustees for neglect of duty, &c., [as provided in the *twentieth* clause of the *twenty-seventh* section of the Consolidated School Act.]—*Scott* v. *Trustees of Union Section No. 1 Burgess and 2 Bathurst.* 19 Q. B. R. 28.

(6.) *Trespass on the School House.*—The Court of Queen's Bench has decided that the trustees of the school, and not the teacher, should sue for a trespass on the school house ; unless it can be shown that the trustees have given the teacher a particular interest in the building, beyond the mere liberty of occupying it during the day for the purpose of teaching. —*Monaghan* v. *Ferguson et al, London.* 3 Q. B. R. 484.

(7.) *The Assessment Act* exempts from taxation "every public school house, with the land attached thereto, and the personal property belonging to it." (Sec. 9, cl. 5.)

NOTE.—See chapter vi on "School Meetings," and section 15 of chapter vii, containing Decision of the Courts in regard to School sites.

III.—POWER AND DUTIES OF TRUSTEES IN REGARD TO THE SCHOOL TEACHERS, &C.

14.—Providing Teacher, Apparatus, Books, School Bell, &c.

The trustees alone, and *not any public meeting*, have the right to decide what teacher shall be employed, how much shall be paid to him ; what apparatus, library, prize and text books shall be purchased ; what repairs ; contingent expenses for stationery, postage, warming and cleaning the school houses, purchase of school bell, &c., shall be authorized, (as explained in section 12 of this chapter;) in short, they alone have the right to decide upon everything which they may think expedient to do in order to promote the interests of the school.

15.—Who shall determine the Expenses of the School.

The majority of the trustees of every school section have, as we have shown, the sole right to decide as to what expenses they will incur for maps, school furniture, apparatus, library and prize books ; salaries of teachers, rent of school house, cost of school bell ; warming cleaning, repairs, contingent and all other expenses of their school. The trustees, as explained in the preceding section, are not required to refer such matters to any public meeting whatever ; and no resolutions of a public meeting on the subject have any legal force, especially as the schools are now "free" by law. (See sec. 1 of chap. xiii.)

16.—Trustees to establish Free Public School Library.

Trustees should, under the general regulations, establish a free public school library for the children and ratepayers of their section. They can appoint and pay any competent person to act as librarian.

In case they do not appoint any such person, the teacher is required, without additional salary, to act as librarian *ex-officio* for the section. (See chapter ix., relating to teachers.)

NOTE.—The property of every public library is exempt from taxation. One hundred per cent. is allowed by the Minister of F .cation on all sums over $1; remitted to the Educational Depository in cor...ction with his Department for library and prize books, maps, apparatus, &c.

17.—Who have a right to attend the School.—Restrictions.

Trustees are required by law to provide school accommodations for all the residents of their section between the ages of five and twenty-one years, whether they attend the school or not. They are also required to admit to their school the children of all resident and adjoining non-resident ratepayers* of their section (between the ages of five and twenty-one years), so long as their conduct is in conformity with the general regulations and the "rules of the school." and so long as the rates or fees required to be paid on their behalf are fully discharged. (See School Act, sec. 102, cls. 8, 19, 20.)

NOTE.—The trustees have authority to admit to their school the children of any other non-residents who are not ratepayers of their section; and they can collect in advance fees or rate-bills from all non-residents, not exceeding fifty cents per calendar month, for admission of such children to the school. (School Act, sec. 102, cl. 20. See also sec. 4 of chap. iv., and secs. 2 and 3 of chap. xiii.)

18.—Authorized Text Books can be alone used.

The School Act makes it the duty of trustees "To see that no unauthorized text books are used in the school, and that the pupils are duly supplied with a uniform series of authorized text books sanctioned and recommended by the Education Department." (Sec. 102, cl. 23.) The Act further declares that "No person shall use any foreign books in the English Branches of education in any model or public school, without the express permission of the Education Department." (*Ibid.* sec. 11; see also sec. 4 of chap. xiii.)

19.—Trustees' Visitation of the School.—Registers, &c.

The Act requires the trustees "to visit, from time to time, every school under their charge, and see that it is conducted according to law and the authorized regulations, and that every such school is, at all times, duly provided, at the expense of the school, with entrance and daily registers and a visitors' book, in the forms prepared according to law." (Sec. 102, cl. 21.) These registers can be obtained through the inspectors gratuitously, or from the Educational Depository on payment of postage. They are also required "to procure annually, for the benefit of their school section, some periodical devoted to education." (Sec. 102. cl. 23.)

* The law declares that the child or children of non-resident ratepayers "shall not be returned as attending any other than the school of the section or division in which the parents or guardians of the child or children reside." (School Act, sec. 160.) The trustees and teacher of a school at which non-resident ratepayers' children attend, must see that the law is complied with in this respect.

NOTE.—The individual power of a trustee in a school is limited. It does not include any right on his part to interfere with the teacher in his administration of discipline in the school, or in his mode of teaching. The teacher is not subject to the direction of an individual trustee, unless acting under the express authority of both of his colleagues. Trustees should not reprove or censure a teacher in the presence of any of his pupils.

20.—Two or more Schools may be established.

Trustees are authorized " to select the site and establish and maintain an additional school or additional schools in the section, with the concurrence of the inspector, where, from the large size of the section, its physical conformation, or from any other cause, the children of the section are unable to attend the school established therein." (Sec. 103, cl. 2.) Under the "compulsory" provisions of the Act this additional school may often be a necessity. (See sec. 2 of chap. viii.)

21.—Duty of Trustees and Teacher to report to the Inspector.

The law declares that a school section shall forfeit its share of the school fund, and the trustees become personally responsible for such loss, should they or the teacher fail to furnish the Inspector with a full and satisfactory report every six months, and at the end of the year, in the form provided. From the instructions printed on the reports themselves, trustees will see that the inspectors are directed to return to them for correction all incomplete or unsatisfactory reports. (Sec. 240.)

22.—Orders to be given to qualified Teachers only.

Trustees are authorized " to give teachers, assistants, or monitors employed by them, the necessary orders upon the County Inspector for the school fund apportioned and payable to their school section," but "they shall not give an order in favour of any teacher (or assistant), except for the actual time during which said teacher, (assistant or monitor,) while employed, held a legal certificate of qualification. (Sec. 102, cl. 18; see also sec. 11 of chap. xiii.)

NOTE.—Trustees sometimes omit the giving of such orders, and thus, designedly or unwittingly, evade the law. They do so for one of four reasons, viz.: (1), if they have themselves advanced the money to the teacher; or (2), have paid him by orders on a store; or (3), if they have employed a teacher without the legal qualifications; or (4), if they wish to aid a male teacher to evade paying the half-yearly superannuation money. In all these cases Inspectors should take steps to prevent it; and whenever they know that a male teacher had been employed in the section, they should deduct from the money payable to the teacher, the super-annuation money payable by him. Under the School Law the Secretary-Treasurer is required to pay over the teacher's superannuation money. (Sec. 102, cl. 1 (5); Sec. 5 of No. 1 (d) next chapter.) Should the trustees pay the teacher in full, without deducting the superannuation money payable by him, they should be called to account. Every order should be made out in favour of the actual teacher employed during the time for which it is issued. (See chapter ix.)

NOTE.—In regard to taking the School Census, see note to Sec. 2, chap. viii.

CHAPTER III.

POWERS AND DUTIES OF A SCHOOL SECRETARY-TREASURER AND COLLECTOR.

1.—Appointment and Duties of a Secretary-Treasurer.

The trustees are required "to appoint a secretary-treasurer who shall give such security as may be required by a majority of the trustees. The trustees shall deposit the security for safe keeping with the township council." (School Act, sec 102, cl. 1.) The object of the appointment of a secretary-treasurer is:—

(1.) *Safety of Papers.*—For "the correct and safe keeping and forthcoming (when called for by the trustees, auditors or other competent authority), of the papers and moneys belonging to the corporation."—*Ibid.*

(2.) *Record of Proceedings.*—For "the correct keeping of a record of all the proceedings of the trustees in a book procured by them for that purpose;"—*Ibid.*

(3.) *Accounts for Moneys.*—For "the receiving and accounting for all school moneys collected by school rate, rate bill, subscription or otherwise from the inhabitants or ratepayers of the school section, or other parties;"—*Ibid.*

(4.) *Payment of Moneys.*—For "the disbursing of such moneys in the manner directed by the majority of the trustees;"—*Ibid.*

(5.) For "the paying over, at the end of every half year, to the order of the Inspector," of the male teacher's superannuation money in his hand.—*Ibid.*

(6.) *Repair of House.*—And for seeing to the repair of the school house, and care of the school premises if desired by the trustees. (See sec. 12 of chap. ii.)

2.—Secretary-Treasurer or Trustee to Account.—Penalty.

Should any secretary-treasurer or trustee wrongfully withhold, neglect or refuse at any time "to deliver up, or to account for and pay over, any books, papers, chattels or moneys which came into his possession as such secretary-treasurer, or trustee or otherwise, * * * or any part thereof to the person, and in the manner directed by a majority of the school trustees for the school section then in office, or by other competent authority, such withholding, neglect or refusal shall be a misdemeanor." (Sec. 231.) And the County Judge is authorized, on the application and affidavit of two trustees or two ratepayers, to direct the delinquent secretary-treasurer, trustee or other person, forthwith "to deliver up, account for or pay over the books, papers, chattels or moneys," in his hands upon pain of imprisonment, without bail, until the order is complied with. (Secs. 232-234.)

3.—Proceedings against a defaulting Secretary-Treasurer.

The Court of Queen's Bench has also decided, that a trustee corporation could maintain an action "for money had and received," against their secretary-treasurer, to recover money in his hands not expended or accounted for. *Trustees of Section 7, Stephen v. Mitchell*, 29 Q. B. R., 382.

4.—Appointment and Duties of a School Collector.

The trustees are required "to appoint some fit and proper person, or one of themselves, to be a collector, who may also be secretary-treasurer." (School Act, sec. 102, cl. 2.)

(1.) Under a warrant from the trustees, the collector is authorised and required to collect the school rates imposed by them, or the sums which the inhabitants or others may have subscribed, and also the school rate bill payable by non-residents. The trustees are authorized to pay the collector at the rate of not less than *five* nor more than *ten* per cent. on the moneys collected by him.—*Ibid.*

(2.) The law gives the collector the same powers (by virtue of a warrant signed by a majority of the trustees) as a township collector, in collecting the school rate, rate bill, or subscription; and it places him under the same liability and obligations.—*Ibid*, sec. 113.

(3.) The collector must proceed in the same manner in his school section and township, as a township collector does in collecting rates in a township or county, as provided in the Municipal Corporation and Assessment Acts which may be in force at the time of collecting the rate.—*Ibid.*

(4.) The collector is required to give such security as may be satisfactory to the trustees, which security shall be lodged with the township council.—(*Ibid*, sec. 102, cl. 2.)

NOTE.—The Collector is entitled to his fee on all school rates entered on the Roll when handed to him by the Trustees, even should any of the rates be paid in to the Trustees, the Secretary or Teacher in the meantime. He must be careful to proceed in strict accordance with the law in the performance of his duty.

5.—Trustee School Rate, or Rate Bill, Roll and Warrant.

The trustees are required to make out, or have made out, from the Township Assessor or Collector's Roll, a list of all persons rated by them for the school purposes of their section. They should annex to such list a warrant directed to the collector of the section, for the collection of the several sums mentioned in such list.* (School Act, sec. 102, cl. 14.)

Where school fees are charged in a rate bill to non-residents, as authorized by law, the following directions should be followed:—

(1.) *Remarks on the Rate Bill.*—As no rate bill on non-residents can exceed 50 cents per calendar month, the whole charge for school fees must be included in this amount. The collector's fees must be paid by the trustees out of the amount collected, or from the general funds of the section. (Sec. 102, cl. 20.)

(2.) To the rate bill should be appended a certificate and warrant by the trustees, similar to those appended to the school rate roll, but varied so as to refer only to school fees.

NOTE.—The form for this Rate Bill can be obtained, free of postage, from Messrs. Copp, Clark & Co., Front Street, Toronto, for 5 cents.

(3.) Rate bills are by law payable in advance. Trustees can, therefore, always make arrangements to pay their teachers punctually. Teachers can, however, make no legal claim for these fees unless the trustees agree beforehand to pay them over to the teachers. They should go into the general funds of the section. (*Ib.*)

(4.) The collector should take a receipt from the secretary-treasurer of the section for all moneys paid to him. The secretary-treasurer should also take a receipt from the teacher for all moneys paid to him. The taking and giving of receipts for moneys paid and received will prevent errors and misunderstandings.

(5.) *Form of a Receipt to Parents or Guardians on the payment of their Rate Bill.*—Received from [*here write the name of the Pupil or Person paying*] the sum of [*here write the sum in words*] in payment of the Rate Bill due from [*here write the name of the Person in whose behalf payment is made*] to the Trustees of School Section No. —, in the Township of ————, for the month ending the — day of ——, 18 .

Dated this — day of ——, 18 .   A. B.,
                         Collector of Common School Moneys [*or Teacher*].

(6.) When the payment of the rate bill is made by the parent or guardian concerned, the receipt should state it accordingly. If payment of the rate bill be made to the teacher, it should be authorized by the trustees. The teacher should, of course, apprize the collector of all payments made to him, so that he (the collector) may not be at the trouble of calling upon such persons.

NOTE.—In regard to non-residents, railways, and other matters, see Directions to Collectors and Decisions of the Courts, &c., further on. (Chap. iv, and sec. 10 of this chapter.)

6.—For what a Section School Rate may be Collected.

A school rate may be lawfully collected for any of the school purposes enumerated in sections 9 to 12, inclusive, of chap. ii.

7.—For what a Section School Rate cannot be Collected.

No rate can be lawfully levied:—

(1. *Teacher's Salary.*)—To pay the salary of any master, assistant teacher, or monitor, who does not, during the whole time for which

---

* Forms of this Rate Roll and Bonds and Security can be supplied by Messrs. Copp, Clark & Co., Front Street, Toronto, free by post, at the following rates:—

Public School Rate Roll with Trustees' Warrant..	6 cents.
Bond of Collector of Public School Rates	5 "
Bond of Secretary-Treasurer	"

the salary is claimed by such teacher, etc., possess a legal certificate of qualification. (School Act, sec. 102, cl. 18.)

(2. *Trustee's Claim.*)—To pay any claim of a co-trustee for anything except a school site, or as remuneration for acting as a collector of school rates. (*Ibid*, sec. 225.)

(3. *Cost of Suits.*)—To pay costs of an illegal suit, or for unsuccessfully defending a suit brought against them for illegal acts. (See decision 10, sec. 12, of this chapter.)

(4. *Unnecessary Expenses.*)—For unnecessary travelling expenses, &c. (See decision (10) of the Courts, section 12, of this chapter.

(5. *For Excessive Interest*,) and the expenses of unauthorized loans, &c.

NOTE.—Persons often illegally refuse to pay school rates levied by trustees, because:—

(1.) A trustee may have omitted to make the declaration of office.

(2.) And because trustees have no school site deed ; but neither of these objections is valid. The law provides other special means of dealing with such cases.

8.—Trustees and the Assessor and Collector's Roll.

The township assessor is required to deliver to the township clerk, not later than the middle of April in each year, his assessment roll, completed and added up. From this roll, as finally approved by the township court of revision,* the clerk is required to make out a township collector's roll. The clerk, or other officer having possession of the assessor or collector's roll, is required to allow any one of the trustees, or their authorized collector, to make a copy of it, so far as it relates to their school section. (Sec. 102, cl. 12 ; secs. 107 and 108 cl. 6.)

9.—Assessors to Value Lands situated in each Section.

The School Law declares that :

(1.) "Whenever the lands or property of any individual or company are situated within the limits of *two* or more school sections, each assessor appointed by any municipality shall assess and return on his roll, separately, the parts of such lands or property, according to the divisions of the school sections within the limits of which such lands or property may be situate.

(2.) "Every undivided occupied lot, or part of a lot, shall only be liable to be assessed for school purposes in the school section where the occupant resides." (Sec. 106. See clause (5) of next section.)

---

* The Assessment Law makes every Municipal Council of five members a Court of Revision : (if over five a court of five must be selected by the Council.) This court is authorized to decide all cases of appeal for over or under assessment, mistakes, omissions or wrongful assessments of every kind. Appeals may be made by any ratepayer, not only in regard to errors in regard to his own assessment but also in regard to that of his neighbours. (Secs. 47-58; see regulations in regard to appeals in note to sec. 6 of chap. xii of these Lectures.)

10.—Guidance of Trustees in framing the Collector's Roll.

(1.) *School Trustees.*—The trustees, in making out their collector's roll must be guided, in regard to the school boundaries, by the school map of the township, in case there should be any dispute. The clerk is required, under a penalty of ten dollars, to make this map, and allow the trustees' assessor or collector to have access to it. They must also adhere strictly to the township assessor or collector's roll in regard to names of persons taxed, and the valuation of their property. (School Act, secs. 107, 108.)

NOTE.—The collector's roll for the school rate must be taken from the township assessor's roll, so far as it relates to the school section. (*Ibid,* sec. 102, cl. 12.)

(2.) *Omission.*—Should any omission or mistake be discovered in the township roll, the council is authorized to correct it, so far as it relates to each school section. (*Ibid.* sec. 107; see note * to sec. 8 of this chapter.)

(3.) *No Omissions.*—The trustees must omit no taxable property in the section from their list; but they may authorize their collector to exempt from payment of the taxes imposed by them, any indigent person in their section. (*Ibid,* sec. 103, cl. 5.)

(4.) *Equalization of Assessment.*—In case of an inequality in the assessment roll of parts of union sections, the reeves (or deputy reeves in the absence of the reeves), and inspector concerned, are required to equalize the assessment of the various parts of such union section every year. (Sec. 135; see note * to sec. 8 of this chapter.)

NOTE.—The mode of equalization is left to the judgment and discretion of the inspector and reeves. The late Chief Justice Robinson (in *Gibson* v. *Huron and Bruce,* 20 Q. B. R. 119), laid down the doctrine that in equalizing the assessment of different townships, "much mus . necessity be left to the judgment of those who have to conduct the operation, and who, by reason of their local knowledge, are best qualified to do so." Further: The legislature "has done the best it could in committing the duty to [the councils] on general terms of equalizing the assessment so as to produce a just relation, but have necessarily left it to them, (as best they can,) to work out the problem." (Page 120. See also the Assessment Act of 1877, Rev. Stat. c. 180, sec. 68; and Part II. of these Lectures.)

(5.) *Undivided Lot.*—In case of an undivided' lot (that is, the whole or a portion of an *original 200 acre lot,* owned by one person), lying in one or more sections, and having the owner or occupant's residence thereon, it must be assessed only in the section in which the occupant resides. (Sec. 106. See (2) of section 9 of this chapter.)

NOTE.—(1.) The "*lot*" here spoken of is one which contained two hundred acres, more or less, according to the original survey, and is occupied by a single individual or company. "*Part of a lot,*" is part of an original two hundred acres lot occupied by a single individual or company. If two or more such parts of a lot should become, at any future time, the property of one person, they must be held from that time to form but part (or the whole) of one lot, in the sense of the Act. (See following decision.)

(2.) *An Undivided Lot must be in the same Municipality—Municipal Boundaries divide Lots.*—The Court of Queen's Bench has decided the following case: Certain property, through which ran a municipal division-line between a town and a town-ship, was assessed by the trustees of a school section in the township, according to the value of that portion of it lying in their section and outside the town. The owner refused to pay, and was sued by the trustees as a non-resident, in accordance with the provisions of the School Law. The Judge of the Division Court decided against the trustees, on the ground that the [*fifty-eighth*] section of the Consolidated School Act referred to undivided lots within different municipalities, as well as within one municipality. The Chief Superintendent appealed the case, and it was held by the court that the trustees acted rightly,—they being guided by the assessment roll of their municipality; and that the proviso referred to applies only to the case of an undivided property extending into more than one school section of the same municipality, and not where the land lies in different municipalities. Hence municipal boundaries divide lots.—*Chief Superintendent of Education, appellant, in re Trustees, No. 4, Hallowell* v. *Storm.* 14 Q. B. R. 541.

6. *Taxes levied equally upon all ratable property.*—The *fifth* section of the Assessment Act provides that "all municipal, local, or direct taxes or rates shall, when no other express provision has been made in this respect, be levied equally upon the whole ratable property, real and personal, of the municipality or other locality, according to the assessed value of such property, and not upon any one or more kinds of property in particular, or in different proportions." Property rates must, therefore, be levied equally on all taxable property of the ratepayers in the section, whether residents or non-residents. (For definition of non-residents' land see chapter iv.) The rate when levied, must be upon all the taxable property in the section (and is a lien upon it), but it must be levied in the name of the individuals mentioned on the assessor's or collector's roll, whether resident or non-resident. (See (8) of section 11, of this chapter.)

(7.) *Rate Bills on Non-Residents.*—No rate bill for fuel, or any other contingency, can be levied on pupils, or on parents or guardians, as such, who own property in the school section. But a rate bill for tuition must be charged for all non-resident children who attend, and whose parents or guardians own no taxable property in the section. (Sec. 102, cl. **20**; see also sec. 5 of this chapter.)

NOTE.—Rate bills (not exceeding twenty cents per month, per pupil) for text books, stationery, fuel and other contingencies, may be collected from parents or guardians in cities, towns and villages. (See School Act, Sec. **105**, cl. **2**.)

(8.) *Owner and Occupant.*—The Assessment of Property Act declares that:—"When land is assessed against both the owner and occupant, or owner and tenant, the assessor shall place both names within brackets on the roll, and shall write opposite the name of the owner the letter F., and opposite the name of the occupant or tenant the letter H. or T.; and both names shall be numbered on the roll, *   *   * and the taxes may be recovered from either, or [if left unpaid] from any future owner or occupant, saving his recourse against any other person." (Assess. Act, section **18**.)

(9.) *Many Owners.*—When land is owned or occupied by more persons than one, and all their names are given to the assessor, they shall be assessed therefor, in the proportion belonging respectively to each; and if a portion of the land so situated is owned by parties who are non-resident, and who have not required their names to be entered on the roll, the whole of the property shall be assessed in the names given to the assessor, saving the recourse of the persons whose names are so given against the others. (Assessment Act, Sec. 19.)

(10.) "·*Unpatented Land*, vested in or held by Her Majesty, which shall hereafter be sold or agreed to be sold to any person, or which shall be located as a free grant, shall be liable to taxation from the date of such sale or grant.   *   *   *   in the same way as other land, whether any license or occupation, location ticket, certificate of sale, or receipt for money paid on such sale, has or has not been, or shall or shall not be issued, and (in case of sale or agreement of sale by the Crown) whether any payment has or has not been, or shall or shall not be, made thereon, and whether any part of the purchase money is or is not overdue and unpaid." (Assess. Act, Sec. 126. For assessment in unorganized townships see chap. xii.)

11.—Duties and Liabilities of Collectors of School Rates.*

These " powers " of, and the mode of "proceeding" observed by township and county collectors, are prescribed in the Assessment of Property Act. Rev. Stat. c. 180. They are adapted to collectors of school rates as follows :—

(1.) *Collector shall call for the Rate.*—The collector, on receiving his warrant and the roll [see page 26], shall call on the party rated, if residing within or near the section, and demand payment ; if a non-resident, he may see him, or send by post a statement of the demand. The entry of the date of such demand on his roll opposite the name, shall be *prima facie* proof of the demand. (Assess. Act, sec. 92.)

(2.) *Shall seize Goods and Chattels of Defaulters.*—In case any person neglects to pay his taxes *fourteen* days after demand made, the school collector may levy the same, with the costs payable to a division court bailiff, by distress of the goods and chattels of the person who ought to pay the same, or of any goods in his possession, wherever the same may be found within the township [or townships] out of which the school section is formed, or of any goods or chattels found on the premises, the property, or in the possession, of any other occupant of the premises. (*Ibid*, 93.)

NOTE.—In the case of non-residents, the same rule applies ; but in default of payment on their part, any goods or chattels found on the premises rated can be seized or sold whether they belong to the non-resident or not. (See clause (8) of this section.)

_____

* For protection of collectors when acting under a lawful warrant, see decisions of Courts of Common Pleas, on pages 17, 33 and 34.

(3.) *Shall give Public Notice and Sell by Auction.*—He shall give notice of the day of sale and the name of the defaulter, in not less than *three* public places in the place where the sale is to be held, at least *six* days before the day of sale, and shall sell by public auction, the property so seized, or so much of it as shall satisfy the debt and costs. (98.) Any person wilfully tearing down, injuring or defacing such notice, or the assessment roll, shall be liable to a fine, before a magistrate, of *twenty dollars*, or twenty days' imprisonment. (*Ibid,* 215.)

(4.) *How to Dispose of Surplus.*—It the property has been sold for more than the rate and costs, and if no claim be made by some other persons on the ground of ownership, lien or other right, he shall return the surplus to the party who was in possession when it was seized, or to such other claimant whose right to it is admitted by the other party. If there be a dispute between them as to the ownership, the surplus shall be paid over to the municipal treasurer until the dispute be settled. (*Ibid,* 97-99.)

(5.) *Liability of Railway Companies in School Sections.*—"The real estate of a railway company (in a school section) *is to be considered as the land of a resident.*" (*Ibid,* 4.) And the company is to transmit annually to the clerk of the municipality, a statement of the value of all their real property within the municipality, the vacant land not in actual use, and the actual value of the land occupied by the road itself; the clerk shall communicate the same to the assessor, and the trustees shall copy it from the assessor's roll and place it upon the collector's roll, with the amount of tax thereon. The collector shall deliver at, or transmit by post to, any station or office of the company, a notice of the total amount at which the trustees have assessed the real property, vacant lands, and the lands occupied by the roadway, and collect the tax at any station or office of the company. (*Ibid,* 26.)

NOTE.—The trustees should send or deliver a bill to the railway company in a form which can be supplied by Messrs. Copp, Clark & Co., free of postage, for 5 cents.

(6.) *Omitted Assessments and Mistakes.*—The School Act authorizes the township council to correct any error in the assessment roll of the section, as certified by the trustees. (Sec. 80; see note * to sec. 8.)

NOTE.—Mistakes, omissions or overcharges in the assessment roll, can also be corrected by the township Court of Revision. (See page 29, and note * to sec 8.)

(7.) *Collector to make Return at the time specified in the Warrant, &c.*—The Collector shall return his roll to the trustees, and pay over the proceeds, within the time fixed in the bond to the trustees, or their warrant to him, otherwise another person may be employed to collect the taxes which the collector does not collect within the time specified. (*Assessment Act,* Secs. 101, 102.)

(8.) *Taxes to be a Special Lien upon Land.*—The taxes accrued on any land shall be a special lien on such land, having preference over any claim, lien, privilege, or incumbrance, of any party except the Crown, and shall not require registration to preserve it. (*Ibid,* 105.)

(9.) *Punishment of Clerks, Assessors or Collectors, making fraudulent Assessments, Collections, &c.*—If any clerk, assessor or collector makes any unjust or fraudulent assessment or collection, or copy of any assessor's or collector's roll, or wilfully and fraudulently inserts therein the name of any person who should not be entered, or wilfully omits any duty required of him by this Act, he shall, upon conviction thereof before a court of competent jurisdiction, be liable to a fine not exceeding *two hundred dollars,* and to imprisonment until the fine be paid, or to imprisonment in the common gaol of the county or city for a period not exceeding *six* months, or to both such fine and imprisonment, in the discretion of the court. (*Ibid,* 191.).

(10.) *Proceedings for compelling Collectors to account for or pay over moneys in their hands.*—If a collector refuses or neglects to pay to the municipal or school treasurer, or other person legally authorized to receive the same, the sums contained in his roll, or duly to account for the same as uncollected, the municipal or school treasurer shall, within twenty days after the time when the payment ought to have been made, issue a warrant under his hand and seal, directed to the sheriff of the county, or the high bailiff of the city, (as the case may be,) commanding him to levy of the goods, chattels, lands and tenements of the collector and his sureties, such sum as remains unpaid and unaccounted for, and to return the warrant within forty days after the date thereof. (*Ibid,* 195.)

12.—Legal Decisions regarding School Rates and Collectors.

(1.) *Collector's Sureties not Responsible for Uncollected Rates, nor for Collector's default, unless they so bind themselves in the bond.*—The Court of Common Pleas has decided the following case :—A person having been duly appointed Collector by the trustees of a school section, s. ned the following contract at the foot of the instrument appointing him : "I agree, &c., &c., to *collect,* &c., according to the said Act, and bind myself, by my securities, in the sum of £250 ;" and immediately under, his sureties signed the following undertaking : " We hereby agree to become security for the due fulfilment of the above contract." The collector paid over a portion of the amount collected by him, leaving a certain sum remaining uncollected. An action was brought by the trustees against the collector and his sureties. *Held,* that the sureties, under their contract, were not jointly liable with their principal for moneys *uncollected* by him ; also, that they were not jointly liable on their guarantee as sureties on default of the principal—the contract only extending to the collection of the rate.—*Trustees No. 6 York* v. *William Hunter et al.*   10 C. P. R. 359.

(2.) *Note of Hand no legal Payment of School Rate.*—The Court of Queen's Bench has decided the following case on a *replevin* [see Index] for horses : *Plea,*—justifying the taking under a warrant for school taxes, and alleging that they were delivered by the collector to defendant, an innkeeper, to take care of until the sale. *Replication,*—setting out facts to show the rate illegal, and averring that plaintiff, after seizure of the goods, at the request of the collector and trustees, gave his note for a sum named, (not saying that it was the amount due by him,) payable to bearer, which was accepted in satisfaction of the taxes ; that the collector released the property seized, and said note is still outstanding, and the plaintiff liable upon it, and that the seizure in the plea mentioned was made afterwards. *Held*, on demurrer, replication bad ; for, 1st, The collector, acting under a warrant legal on the face of it, would not be liable in trespass or trover, and therefore not in this action, nor the defendant for taking the horses from him to keep ; and, 2nd, Even if the note had been for a sufficient amount to pay the rate, yet the improper acceptance of it by the trustees would not prevent them from afterwards distraining.—*Spry v. McKenzie.*   18 Q. B. R. 161.

(3.) *Extension of time for collecting School Rates.—Duration of Collector's authority.*—The Court of Queen's Bench has decided the following case: The time for levying a school tax in the city of Kingston, imposed by by-law in December, 1855, was extended by resolutions of the city council, under 18 Vic. c. 21, s. 3, until the 1st of August, 1856; and again, on the 22nd of December, 1856, to the 1st of March, 1857. *Held*, that the collector, who was the same person for both years, might distrain between the 1st of August and the 22nd of December, 1856, although no resolution extending the time was then in force—*McLean, J.*, dissenting.—*Newberry v. Stephens et al, City of Kingston.*   16 Q. B. R. 65.

NOTE.—As a doubt was expressed by one Judge in this case as to the legality of the extension of time, it would be better for trustees to issue a new warrant and take a fresh bond whenever the period mentioned in the bond expires.

(4.) *Right to collect School Taxes after the expiration of the Year.*—The Court of Queen's Bench has decided, on an appeal by the Chief Superintendent of Education, that a collector of school taxes might, in 1861, collect by distress the taxes for 1859 and 1860, not having made his final return of such taxes as in arrear, and being still collector ; and *semble*, that in this case the plaintiff, who complained of the seizure, having led to it by his own conduct, the proceeding should have been upheld in the division court at all events.—*Chief Superintendent of Education, appellant, in re McLean v. Farrell.*   21 Q. B. R. 441.

(5.) *Collector committing Trespass is entitled to Notice of Action.—Limit.*—The Court of Common Pleas has decided that a collector who committed a trespass while acting under a warrant issued by a competent authority, was entitled to notice of action, and that the action should be brought within six months.—*Spry v. Mumby, et al, No. 15, Rawdon.*   11 C. P. R. 285.

(6.) *School Trustees have power to levy Rate at any time.*—Under the Acts relating to Public Schools, trustees may *at any time* impose and levy a rate for school purposes ; they are not bound to wait until a copy of the revised assessment roll for the particular year has been transmitted to the clerk of the municipality, but may and can use the existing revised assessment roll.—*Chief Superintendent of Education, appellant, in re Hogg v. Rogers.*   15 C. P. R. 417.

(7.) *Expenses of the School must be defrayed by the authority of the Trustees, and not by the inhabitants themselves.*—The Court of Queen's Bench has decided that freeholders and householders of a school section cannot substitute a voluntary subscription among themselves, and a rate upon the parents and guardians of children alone, for the whole expenses of the school, instead of the provisions made by law ; and a resolution to have such private subscription, which the trustees neglected to collect, is therefore no answer to an avowry by the trustees of a rate levied by them in the usual way.—*McMillan v. Rankin et al, No. 14, Kingston.*   19 Q. B. R. 356.

(8.) *School Tax upon Parents and Guardians unlawful.*—The Court of Common Pleas has also decided a similar case : A general school meeting passed the following resolution : "That the expenses of the school section be paid by voluntary subscription, and the balance to be raised from a *tax to be levied upon the parents and guardians* of those sending children to school." The school trustees, after the failure of the voluntary subscription, levied a general rate, upon which this replevin arose—the plaintiff contending that he was not liable, as *not being a parent of guardian* of a child attending the school. *Held*, that the trustees had no authority to tax the parents or guardians of those sending children, or to alter or annul the resolutions; and that the *tenth* clause of the *twenty-seventh* section of the School Act authorized the levy as made.—*Craig* v. *Rankin et al, No. 14 Kingston.* 10 C. P. R. 186.

(9.) *Form of, and number of, Signatures to Trustees' Warrant.*—The Court of Queen's Bench has decided that the warrant may be signed by two trustees [with the knowledge of the third]. In making cognizance under this warrant, it is sufficient to state that the plaintiff was duly assessed, and that the collector was duly appointed. It is not necessary to state therein that the rate was decided upon at a meeting, as required by statute, or how the appointment of collector was made.—*Gillies* v. *Wood, No. 6, Pilkington.* 13 Q. B. R. 357.

(10.) *No Rate can be imposed by Trustees for the reimbursement of costs in defending Illegal Acts.*—The Court of Queen's Bench has decided that trustees cannot impose a rate to reimburse themselves for costs incurred in defending unsuccessfully a suit brought against them for levying an unauthorized rate, or for travelling expenses incurred in order to consult with the superintendent; but a rate may be levied to reimburse school trustees for the costs of defending a *groundless* action brought against them.—*Chief Superintendent of Education, appellant, in re Stark* v. *Montague,* 14 Q. B. R. 473; and *Tiernan* v. *Municipality of Nepean,* 15 Q. B. R. 87.

(11.) *Mandamus against Clerk of a Township to permit Trustees to examine the Assessment Roll.*—The Court of Queen's Bench has decided that where, on an application for a mandamus, a demand and a refusal were sworn to, and defendant in answer denied the refusal, and alleged that he had always been willing to do what was required, the Court nevertheless granted the writ.—*In re Trustees of Union School Section Nos. 15, Otonabee, 10, Douro, and 11, Asphodel* v. *Casement,* 17 Q. B. R. 275.

NOTE.—A *mandamus* is a command issuing in the name of the Sovereign from a superior court having jurisdiction, and is directed to some person, corporation, or inferior court, within the jurisdiction of such superior court, requiring them to do some particular thing therein specified, which appertains to their office and duty, or to show cause why they have not done it. This writ was introduced to prevent disorders from a failure of justice: therefore it ought to be used upon all occasions where the law has established no specific remedy, and where, in justice and good government, there ought to be one.

(12.) *Testator's Estate liable for School Rate in the hands of Devisees and Executors.*—The Court of Common Pleas decided as follows:—An action of replevin may be brought upon a distress for school rates, and notice of action is not necessary, where several devisees and executors were rated for a school rate in respect to the property of their testators as "John Applegarth and brothers," which entry appeared to have been made at the instance of some of them; but two of them only had slept on the premises occasionally, although such was not their ordinary place of residence, and they had received the usual notice of assessment in the form without appealing, and the same two had paid taxes on an assessment on the township roll in their individual names. *Held*, by the Court:—1st, That the facts afforded sufficient evidence to show that the plaintiffs were "inhabitants" for the purposes of the rate; 2nd, That the parties were sufficiently named on the roll to render the rate lawful; 3rd, That a demand made by the collector on "John Applegarth," named on the roll, was sufficient to bind all the plaintiffs.—*Applegarth et al,* v. *Graham, No. 3. Flamborough East.* 7 C. P. R. 171. (See "Non-Residents," chapter iv.)

(13.) *Liability of Executors and Devisees.*—The Court of Queen's Bench has decided that where executors and devisees in trust of land were assessed as owners: *Held*, that they were properly so assessed, and that their own goods might be seized for the taxes.—*Dennison* v. *Henry.* 17 Q. B. R. 276.   **3**

(14.) *Overrated Taxes paid cannot be recovered back.*—The Court of Queen's Bench has decided that, if a person overrated pay the overrate without remonstrance or compulsion, he cannot afterwards recover it back. *Grantham* v. *City of Toronto*, 2 Q. B. R. 475.

(15.) *Other cases cited.*—The following cases amongst others also bear upon the question of local municipal rates : *Ridsdale* v. *Brush*, (Roman Catholic Separate School case,) 22 Q. B. R. 122 ; *Fraser* v. *Page*, (general powers, etc.,) 18 Q. B. R. 336 ; *Holcolm* v. *Shaw*, (who ought to pay the taxes ?) 22 Q. B. R. 92 ; also *Squire* v. *Mooney*, 30 Q. B. R. 531 ; *Jarvis* v. *Cayley*, (error in sale,) 11 Q. B. R. 282 ; *Coleman* v. *Kerr*, (affirming (3) on page 34,) 27 Q. B. R. 5 ; *Secretary of War* v. *Toronto*, (lien on land,) 22 Q. B. R. 555 ; *McBride* v. *Gardham*, (affirming (3) above page 34,) 8 C. P. R. 296 ; *Anglin* v. *Minis*, (validity of one demand not affected by change of occupant,) 18 C. P. R. 170 ; *Berlin* v. *Grange*, (non-residents,) 5 C. P. R. 211.

13.—Application to Township Council to Collect Rates.

Before collecting any school rate, the trustees should decide before hand whether the money required by them for any purpose should be collected (1) by themselves, (2) by the township council, or (3) raised by loan, under the authority of the council. In case either the second or third mode be decided upon, an estimate of the sum required by the trustees should be sent to the township council, at or before its August meeting. (Sec. 47.) Should the second mode be decided on, the council, upon receiving the trustees' estimate, and a request in writing, must levy the whole of the required rate within a reasonable time, and pay it over to the trustees, (without any diminution of collector's fees or expenses—which must be added to the rate by the council.) Should the third mode be decided on, the council may grant the required permission at its discretion. Should the council do so, it must issue a debenture for the sum to be borrowed, and provide the means for securing repayment of the amount borrowed, by a yearly rate imposed in the manner specified in the Act. (See clauses 8 to 11 inclusive; see also chap. i. sec. 8, cl. (*f*), note of these lectures.)

NOTE.—In the chapter in Part II. of these Lectures, on Township Councils, full directions will be found in regard to the mode of providing for the school loans.

14.—Township Council required to raise Money for Trustees.

The School Law declares that every township council shall levy by assessment upon the taxable property in any school section, such sum as may be required by the trustees thereof "for the purchase of a school site; the erection, repair, rent, furniture and fittings of a school house and its appendages, the erection and repair of fences, outbuildings, or the rent or purchase of maps, apparatus, text, library and prize books for the school, and salary of the teacher, assistant or monitor, as may be determined by such trustees." (Sec. 78, cl. 8.)

NOTE.—In case of refusal, on the part of a township council, to levy the amount required by the trustees, the remedy is by mandamus from either the Court of Queen's Bench or Common Pleas. (Decisions of the Courts on this subject are given in Part II. of these Lectures, and also an analysis of the whole school law in regard to township councils.)

CHAPTER IV.

THE LAW RELATING TO NON-RESIDENTS.

1.—A Resident of a School Section Defined.

(1.) A person who has his home, domicile, or place of business in a section or other school division, and on which he pays taxes, is a resident ratepayer, and, as such, is eligible to be elected a trustee; (2.) Apprentices; (3.) Railway Companies having roadways, stations, &c., in a section or other school division, and (4.) *bona fide* settlers whose names are not yet on the assessment roll, are to be regarded as residents. (See clause (12) of section 11, of chapter iii.)

2.—A Non-Resident of a School Section Defined.

A "non-resident" of a school section or division, is, strictly speaking, one who does not reside in it. But a person may be a school ratepayer of a section, and have the right to send to its school, and yet not reside in it. Transient visitors, and children who leave home and come to remain in a section or division for a period under twelve months, are also non-residents.

3.—Non-Residents Liable for Rates in their own Section.

A person paying rates in the section in which he resides does not thereby relieve himself from the payment of rates in any other school section in which he owns property and is taxed. (Sch. Act, sec. 160.)

NOTE.—Although the children of such a person attend the school of a neighbouring section in which he pays rates, yet their attendance must be returned only in the section in which they reside.—(*Ibid.* See next section, and also secs. 3 & 4, chap. xiii.)

4.—Rights of the Non-Resident Ratepayers of a Section.

A non-resident ratepayer of a section (as defined above) has a right to send his children, or wards (if he be a guardian), to the school of any section in which he pays school rates; but such children "shall not be returned as attending any other than the school in the section, or division, in which the parents or guardians of the child or children reside." (*Ibid*, sec. 160. See next section.)

NOTE.—Any resident claiming to be the guardian of a non-resident or other child that may come to live with him, must satisfy the trustees, by documentary other legal proof, of the validity of his claim to be such guardian.

5.—Authority of Trustees in regard to Non-Residents.

Trustees may, at their discretion, admit the children of non-residents to their school on payment in advance of fifty cents per child per calendar month. Should the non-residents reside nearer to the school than to the one in their own section, the trustees must admit them on the payment of the fee. In case of any dispute as to the comparative distance from the school, the inspector has power to finally decide the matter. (Sec. 102, cls. 19, 20.)

NOTE.—Supporters of Roman Catholic separate schools, have no right to send their children to the public schools while they are supporters of these schools.

6.—Definition of the words "Lands of Non-Residents."

The Assessment Act declares that "unoccupied land shall be denominated 'Lands of Non-residents,' unless the owner thereof has a legal domicile or place of business in the local municipality where the same is situate, or gives notice in writing, setting forth his full name, place of residence and post office, to the clerk of the municipality," etc. (Assess. Act, sec. 3; see also cl. 8 of sec. 9, chap. iii.)

7.—How is Land not occupied by the Owner, to be assessed?

The same Act says: "As to land not occupied by the owner, but of which the owner is known, and who, at the time of the assessment being made, resides, or has a legal domicile or place of business in the municipality, or who has given the notice mentioned in the [preceding] section six, the same shall be assessed against such owner alone, if the land is unoccupied, or against the owner and occupant, if such occupant be any other person than the owner." (*Ibid*, sec. 15.)

8.—How is Land Assessed when the Owner is unknown?

Further, the Act says: If the owner of the land be not resident, then, if the land is occupied, it shall be assessed in the name of and against the occupant and owner, but if the land be not occupied, and the owner has not requested to be assessed therefor, then it shall be assessed as land of a non-resident. (*Ibid*, sec. 16.)

9.—How to collect Rates from Non-Residents.

(1.) *Assess Non-Residents.*—Non-residents owning taxable property in the section should be assessed as other ratepayers. The collector shall, *one* month after delivery to him of the roll and warrant, and *fourteen* days after he has transmitted by post a statement and demand, levy for the amount due (with costs, same as payable to a division court bailiff), and make "distress of the goods and chattels of the person who ought to pay the same, or of any goods or chattels in his possession, wherever the same may be found within * * * the local municipality, or of any goods or chattels *found on the premises,* the property of, or in the possession *of, any other occupant of the premises;* and no claim of property, lien, or privilege shall be available to prevent the sale, or the payment of the taxes and costs out of the proceeds thereof." He shall then advertise and sell, as in the case of other defaulters. (*Ibid*, secs. 93-95; see sec. 10 of chap. iii.)

(2.) *Chattels.*—In case, after diligent enquiries, no goods or chattels can be found on the land in the section, or on any land of the owner in the township, and the resident lives near or is known, and still refuses payment of the rate (or in case a person assessed moves out of the section and refuses payment), the trustees must sue such person in the division court.   (School Act, sec. 102, cl. 15.)

(3.) *Return to Clerk.*—In case the non-resident school rate cannot be collected by the trustees, and it is not known where the delinquent non-resident lives, the trustees are required, before the end of the year, to make a return to the clerk of the municipality of the lands of such non-residents, with a statement of the uncollected taxes due on them.   The municipal council is then required (after the beginning of the next year) to pay those taxes to the trustees out of the general funds of the municipality.   In case of refusal to do so, the council can be sued by the trustees for the amount.   (School Act, sec. 102, cl. 16; sec. 108, cl. 4.)

NOTE.—The true and effectual remedy for the inconvenience arising out of the "non-resident" relation which a school section system entails (with its law of restricted boundaries and school fees), is the adoption of a Township Board system, as provided by law.

10.—Legal Decisions in regard to Non-Residents' Taxes.

(1.) *Mode of collecting School Rates from Residents and Non-Residents.*—The Court of Queen's Bench has decided that trustees are bound to collect by warrant from the *residents* of the school section; and to sue for and recover by their name of office from persons residing without the limits of the section and making default of payment.—*Chief Superintendent of Education, appellant, in re Trustees, 2 Moore v. Wm. McRae*, 12 Q. B. R. 525.   (See note to next clause.)

(2.) *Trustees' Warrant to collect School Rates only legal within their own Section. They must sue non-residents.*—The Court of Queen's Bench has also decided that school trustees can only issue a warrant to collect school rates within the limits of the section for which they are appointed.—*Gillies v. Wood, No. 6, Pilkington.* 13 Q. B. R. 357.

NOTE.—This decision was virtually confirmed in 1870 by the Court of Common Pleas in the case of *Chief Superintendent in re Chapman* v. *Thrasher et al*, (20 C. P. R. 259,) with the addition of one of defining that a collector's municipality was a school section beyond which his jurisdiction did not extend.   The School Act of 1871, however, declares that a school collector "shall have the same power and proceed in the same manner *in his school section and township*, as a township collector, in collecting rates in a township or county."

(3.) *Return of uncollected non-resident rates of past years may be made by Trustees. Such rates are payable immediately out of the general funds of the township.*—The Court of Common Pleas has decided that, by the School Law, it is made the duty of the local municipality to make up and supply any deficiency arising to the school fund which arises from the inability of the collector of school rates to collect the same by reason of there being no resident on such land, or no goods and chattels thereon which can be distrained; and that the Legislature intended that such deficiency should be made up out of the general funds of the municipality, immediately after the return made to the clerk of the municipality of what school rates are so in arrear.   It was also held that trustees may, before the end of each current year, return all school rates upon lands not collected for the reasons stated in the Act, and of which no prior return has been made to the clerk of the municipality.—*School Trustees No. 1, Arthur v. Township Council of Arthur and Luther.* 9 C. P. R. 532.

(4.) *Mandamus not granted when other remedies can be had.*—The Court of Common Pleas has decided that, as a general rule, a mandamus will not be granted unless the party making the application has no other specific legal remedy [*i.e.*, by suit (as in the case under review) of the trustees to recover imposed school rates on lands of non-residents.] Upon an application by school trustees for a mandamus to obtain money from a municipal corporation, the affidavits being contradictory, and this court having decided in the case of *School Trustees of Arthur* v. *The Municipality of Arthur*, 9 C. P. R. 532 [quoted above], that an action for a balance due on a case such as this would lie, the mandamus was refused.—*School Trustees No. 7, Elzevir* v. *The Municipality of Elzevir*. 12 C. P. R. 548.

NOTE.—In case of refusal on the part of the township council to pay the amount of these uncollected rates, duly returned to its clerk before the end of the year in which the rate was levied, the trustees can at once enter an action against the township council for such amount.

(5.) *Executors, equally with the Testators, liable for School Rate on Non-Resident's Land.*—The Court of Common Pleas has decided that a resolution of the freeholders and householders of a school section to pay the teacher's salary and the expenses of the school, followed by a resolution of the trustees, directing a rate to be delivered on the rateable property of such section, to raise the sum required, and the preparation of a rate bill and warrant, are sufficient to render a non-resident, having real estate within the section, liable for the sum rated by the trustees, according to the assessed value of his real property : and that, being so liable, an executor representing the estate is liable in an action of the same nature to which the testator might have been subjected.—*Trustees No. 2, Dunwich* v. *McBeath*, 4 C. P. R. 228. (See clauses (12) and (13) of section 11, chapter iii.)

CHAPTER V.

SCHOOL SECTION AUDITORS—ACCOUNTABILITY OF TRUSTEES AND OTHERS.

1.—When and by whom School Auditors are appointed.

The law requires the trustees of each section to appoint " a fit and proper person " to be auditor of their school accounts *before the first of December* in each year. In case of their neglect to do so, or in case the one appointed refuses to act, the inspector shall appoint one for them. The ratepayers are also required, *at each annual meeting*, to appoint another auditor, so that either auditor, or the two together, may audit the trustees' accounts. (Sec. 51, cl. 4 ; and sec. 102, cl. 3.)

2.—Auditors' Time of Meeting, and object of it.

The auditors chosen, or either of them, shall, " on or after the first day of December, in each year, forthwith appoint a time before the day of the next annual meeting for examining the accounts of the school section." They should, of course, apprize the trustees of the fact. (Sec. 115.)

3.—The object of the School Audit, and duty of the Auditors

Is " to examine into and decide upon the accuracy of the accounts of such section, and whether the trustees have truly accounted for,

and expended for school purposes, the moneys received by them."
(School Act, sec. 118, cl. 1.)

4.—Duration of the Time of the Audit.

In case of delay in completing the audit, even beyond the year of
appointment, the law declares that "the auditors shall remain in
office *until their audit is completed.*" (*Ibid*, sec. 118, cl. 4.)

5.—When, and to whom, are the Auditors to Report.

The auditors are required "to submit" the school accounts of the
section, "with a full report thereon, to the next annual school meeting." They, or either of them, are further required to report at the
same time "the result of their or his examination of the accounts of
the year," and, with the trustees, to sign with the trustees the annual
school report for presentation to the meeting. (See School Act, sec.
118, cl. 2; and sec. 119, cl. 4; also sec. 3 of this chapter.)

6.—What the School Auditors have authority to do.

The School auditors can "require the attendance of all, or any of
the parties interested in the accounts, and of their witnesses, with all
such books, papers and writings as such auditor or auditors may
direct them, or either of them, to produce." The auditors may
"administer oaths to such parties and witnesses." They have also
full power to enforce by warrant the collection of any moneys by
them awarded to be paid. (School Act, sec. 119.)

7.—Obligation on Trustees and others to furnish Information.

The law declares that "if the trustees, or their secretary-treasurer,
in their behalf, refuse to furnish the auditors of any accounts of a
rural school section, or either of them, with any papers or information
in their power, and which may be required of them, relative to their
school accounts, the party refusing shall be guilty of a misdemeanor,
and upon prosecution [before a magistrate] by either of the auditors
or any ratepayer, shall be punished by fine or imprisonment."
(*Ibid.* sec. 239.)

8 —Obligations on Trustees and other parties to Account.

The School Act also declares, that if any secretary-treasurer, school
trustee, or other person who may have in his possession any books,
papers, chattels or moneys, or into whose hands any school moneys
or school property shall come, who wrongfully withholds or neglects
or refuses to account for or deliver up the same, when called upon by
a majority of the trustees, a school auditor or auditors, or other competent authority to do so, the County Judge shall order the party complained of to deliver up, account for and pay over, the books, papers,
chattels or moneys applied for, by a certain day, with reasonable

costs, on pain of imprisonment by the sheriff, without bail. (*Ibid*, secs. 231-235.)

9.—Responsibility of Trustees and others for Lost Moneys.

If it can be proved at the audit, or at any other time, that "any part of the public school money be embezzled or lost, through the dishonesty or faithlessness of any trustee, secretary-treasurer, or other person to whom it has been entrusted, and proper security against the loss not having been taken, the person or persons whose duty it was to have exacted the security shall be *personally responsible* for the sum so embezzled or lost; and such sum may be recovered from him or them by the party entitled to receive the same, by action at law in any court having jurisdiction to the amount, or by information at the suit of the Crown." (*Ibid*, sec. 230; see *Ferris* v. *Irwin*, No. 16 Darlington, 10 C.P.R., 116, in regard to Embezzlement by Trustees.)

10.—"Lawfulness" or Expediency of Trustees' Expenditure.

The auditors may object to the *lawfulness*, but not to the expediency of any expenditure. The trustees are the sole judges as to the *expediency* of such expenditure. It is only when both of the auditors object to the lawfulness of an expenditure, or when the auditors differ between themselves as to the *lawfulness* of the expenditure, (that is, whether the expenditure is authorized by the School Law, or comes fairly within the objects of the trust,) that it is necessary to submit the matter for the decision of the school meeting, and finally to the chief superintendent or inspector. (See sec. 118 of School Act, and next section of this chapter.)

11.—What are Lawful School Section Expenditures?

The "expenditure" of a school may be "for any lawful purpose whatsoever," and may not only include the ordinary expenses of the school, but also collector's fees, law costs incurred in maintaining or defending necessary suits, postages, stationery, or any incidentals connected with the office of trustees.

NOTE.—While trustees carry out the lawful decision of their constituents, neither the ai ' ors nor any public meeting can limit or deprive them of the authority confer: r upon them by the Act, "as to whatever they may judge expedient with regard to the building, repairing, renting, warming, furnishing, and keeping in order the section school house, and its furniture and appendages, and the school lands and enclosures held by them ; and procuring apparatus, library, prize and text books for their schools, &c.," as mentioned in section 15 of chapter ii. (See also sections 6 and 7 of chapter iii.)

12.—Summary in regard to Audit of School Section Accounts.

The law requires trustees, their secretary-treasurer and all other parties concerned, to "furnish the school section auditors with all vouchers for the payment of school money during the year, together with such contracts, agreements, papers, books, &c., and verbal information, under oath, if necessary, on the subject of the receipts and expe. liture, as may serve to explain the items in the accounts. In case of difference of opinion between the auditors on any matters in the accounts, it shall be referred to and decided by the county inspector." (School Act, secs. 114 and 118.)

13.—Summary of Duties of Rural School Trustees.*

The duties which trustees are required to perform, as well as their discretionary powers, may be summarized as follows :—

(1.) To call the annual school meeting, and also a special one in case of any difference in regard to the school site, death or removal of trustees, &c.

(2.) To call school meetings when desired by the ratepayers to decide the question of school site.

(3.) To call a special school meeting for any lawful school purpose.

(4.) To prosecute all illegal voters at school meetings.

(5.) To make a verbal declaration of office within *two* weeks after notice or knowledge of election as trustee.

(6.) To see that their school is furnished with a trustees' book, a visitors' book, teachers' daily and general registers, and a *Journal of Education*. The three former must be purchased at the expense of the school.

(7.) To appoint a person to make an annual return of all the children in their school section or division who do not attend any school.

(8.) To charge absentee pupils not more than one dollar per month for such absence, or report the case to a magistrate.

(9.) To provide suitable school accommodation for all the pupils in their section, as defined in the regulations.

(10.) To employ and pay school moneys to none but legally qualified teachers, assistants or monitors.

(11.) To fix a rate bill, not exceeding fifty cents each, per calendar month, (payable in advance,) upon the children of non-residents who are sent to their school.

(12.) To permit all pupils between the age of five and twenty-one years, on whose behalf school rates are paid, and who observe the ru! , to attend their school.

(13.) To visit the school and see that it is properly conducted; that no unauthorized books are used; that all the pupils are properly supplied with proper text books.

* The provision of the law prescribing the duty of trustees in regard to compulsory education, will be found in chapter viii.

(14.) To exercise all the corporate powers vested in them, for the fulfilment of all agreements, contracts, &c.; and to maintain a school in their section during the year.

(15.) To transmit their *half-yearly* returns and their *yearly* reports to the inspector, and also to submit their *yearly* report to the annual meeting of their constituents.

(16.) To affix their corporate seal to all contracts, agreements, deeds, &c., under their hand.

(17.) To appoint and take proper security from the secretary-treasurer and school collector.

(18.) To make a return to the municipal clerk of all rates imposed by them.

(19.) To make no contract with any member of the school corporation, except for school site, or as collector.

(20.) To transact no school business except at a trustee meeting, of which each member of the corporation has had due notice.

(21.) To appoint a school auditor before the 1st of December in each year, and lay before the auditors all necessary information.

(22.) To comply with the award of the arbitrators arising between themselves and other parties, under the school law.

(23.) To provide, at the expense of the section, for the cleaning of the school house and the lighting of fires, &c.

(24.) To provide a well, play yard and separate conveniences for boys and girls.

(25.) To provide an assistant for their school, in case the number of enrolled pupils exceeds fifty.

(26.) To see that the prescribed programme is fully carried out.

(27.) To establish a free public school library as required by law, to see that it is available to the inhabitants, and that it is properly managed.

(28.) To follow the township assessor's roll in making out the list of, and collecting, the school rate.

(29.) To take possession and have sole custody of all public school property, movable property, moneys, &c.

(30.) To obtain a legal title to their school premises, as provided by law, and register the same of the award of arbitrators.

(31.) To do whatever they may judge expedient in regard to the building, fitting, &c., of the school house, appendages, play ground, enclosures, lands, and movable property.

(32.) To have the sole authority to appoint by written agreement, and fix the amount of the salary of all male and female teachers employed by them.

(33.) To provide a teacher's residence.

(34.) To appoint a school collector, secretary-treasurer, &c.

(35.) To establish, if they judge expedient (with the consent of the inspector), two or more schools in their section.

(36.) To raise all moneys required for their school as they may see fit.

(37.) To apply, if they judge expedient, to the township council once a year, before the August meeting (except in case of a site and building), to raise any school rate required by them, and to compel the council to collect it, by *mandamus* from one of the Superior Courts, should the council refuse to do so.

(38.) To exempt at their pleasure all indigent persons from section school rates, and provide their children with text books.

(39.) To sue non-residents for school rates or school fees. School taxes on absentees must, however, be collected as pointed out in section 9, chapter iv. In case the township council should refuse to pay these taxes (duly returned to the clerk), the trustees can enter an action, in any competent court, against the township council for the amount.

(40.) To resign the office of trustee (if necessary), with the consent in writing of their colleagues and of the inspector.

(41.) To decline re-election if they see fit for *four* years next after going out of office.

(42.) To apply to county council against any objectionable act or by-law of a township council in altering the boundaries of the school, or to request an adjustment of their school section boundaries.

(43.) To comply with the school law and regulations generally.

N.B.—No school meeting of their constituents can deprive trustees of any of these powers, or prevent their exercise.

CHAPTER VI.
PUBLIC SCHOOL MEETINGS.

1.—Day of Annual School Meeting fixed by Law.

The day fixed by statute for the annual school meetings throughout the province is the second Wednesday of January, and the hour at ten o'clock in the forenoon. The proceedings cannot close before eleven o'clock, nor be kept open after four o'clock P.M. of that day. They cannot stand over to the following day, nor be adjourned, nor fail, should only four ratepayers be present. (School Act, secs. 39 and 41 ; see also next section of this chapter.)

2.—Public Notice of Meeting must be given by Trustees.

Three public notices, to be posted in as many conspicuous places in the school section, should be issued at least six clear days before the day of meeting, and signed by the secretary (by direction of the trustees), or by a majority of the trustees themselves. The corporate seal need not be attached to them. These notices should state the *time* and *place* of meeting, and all the business to be brought forward. Should the meeting fail to be held for want of notice on the part of the trustees, or other cause, any two ratepayers, or the inspector, may call a school meeting within twenty days after the second Wednesday of January. (School Act, sec. 102, cl. 25.)

NOTE.—The foregoing relates to cases in which trustees refuse or neglect to call the annual meeting ; but in case of inadvertence, or error, the trustees can at once call the meeting themselves, or authorize their secretary to do so.

3.—Who are, and who are not, School Electors of a Section.

Every school ratepayer of the section, whether resident or non-resident, female or minor, who has paid a county, township or section school tax during the year, and who is not a supporter of a separate school, has a right to be present and vote at a school meeting. (*Ibid*, secs. 51 and 52.)

4.—Declaration of School Section Elector's Right to Vote.

In case any one objects to an elector's right to vote, the chairman should require the elector to make a declaration to that right in the following form (on doing so, his vote must be received without further question):—

"I do declare and affirm that I have been rated on the assessment roll of this school section as a freeholder (householder, or tenant, *as the case may be*), and that I have paid a public school tax due by me in this school section, imposed within the last *twelve* months, and that I am legally qualified to vote at this meeting." (*Ibid*, sec. 52.)

NOTE.—This "public school tax" may be a county, township or section one. In new school sections the payment of a county tax alone is required.

5.—Chairman and Secretary of the School Meeting.

The first thing to be done, before proceeding to other business, is the appointment of a chairman and secretary. The chairman may be an elector or non-elector, at the pleasure of the meeting (if a non-elector he cannot vote). The secretary may be the teacher of the section, or any other competent person. (See sec. 11 of this chapter.)

6.—Duties of the Chairman of a School Meeting.

(1.) To keep order.

(2.) To decide all questions of order, subject to an appeal to the meeting.

(3.) To give a casting vote (but no other) if an elector.

(4.) To take the votes on any question before the meeting, in any manner desired by two electors present. (See clause (1) and note to clause (2), section 9; and also section 14 of this chapter.)

(5.) To require any elector, whose right to vote is questioned, to make the declaration prescribed by the statute. (See sec. 4 above.)

NOTE—The chairman has no right to declare any vote bad unless the voter refuses to make the foregoing declaration ; nor has he any right to receive any protest against the legality of the meeting or its proceedings. That must be made to the Inspector. (See note to sec. 2, also clause (3) of sec. 9, of this chapter.)

(6.) To hear the verbal declaration of office made (in the words of the statute) by the trustee elect. (See sec. 4 of chap. i.)

(7.) To transmit to the inspector a copy of the proceedings of the meeting, signed by himself and the secretary, under a penalty of five dollars for neglecting to do so. (School Act, secs. 46, 47 and 50.)

7.—Duties of the Secretary of a School Meeting.

(1.) To make a correct minute of the proceedings.

(2.) To record the votes of the electors (if desired by the chairman).

(3.) To sign the minutes for transmission to the inspector.

(4.) To hear the declaration of office made by the chairman, in case he should be elected trustee. (*Ibid.* secs. 19, 45 and 50.)

8.—Prescribed Order of Business at a School Meeting.

The following is the order in which the business of an annual school meeting should be taken up. (School Act, sec. 51):—

(1.) Calling the meeting to order by the senior trustee present.

(2.) Election of chairman and secretary.

(3.) Reading of the trustees' annual report and auditors' statement of receipts and expenditure. (See section 12 of this chapter.)

(4.) Reception of trustees' report and auditors' statement.

NOTE.—The school meeting has no legal power to object, or pass any resolution in regard, to the amount of any proposed expenditure by the trustees for the current year, nor to interfere with them in their appointment of the teacher or assistant, or the fixing of his or their salary. The expenses of the school must be held to include the items of rent, insurance, repairs, fittings, printing; salary of teacher; maps, apparatus, tablets, library, prize and text books; fuel, cleaning, lighting fires, care of premises; postage, stationery; collector's fees; cost of site, building, teacher's residence, outbuildings, shed, fence, school bell; planting and laying out grounds ; and all other necessary outlays incurred by trustees in efficiently maintaining the school. (See sec. 14 of chapter ii.)

(5.) Election of trustee to fill the vacancy of the year. (See sec. 13.)

(6.) Election of trustee or trustees to fill any other vacancy.

(7.) Election of a school auditor for the next year.

(8.) Any other business of which due notice had been given.

NOTE.—No business can be lawfully transacted at a school meeting, unless due notice shall have been given of it by the trustees, inspector, &c., beforehand.

9.—Rules to be observed at each School Meeting.

The following rules are to be observed at each school meeting (see also section 10 of this chapter), viz.:

(1.) *Poll demanded.*—The names of those who vote for, and of those who vote against, a motion, shall be entered upon the minutes, if two electors require it, at the time of voting, and even after the chairman has declared the motion carried. (See section 14, below.)

(2.) *Four* 'll votes shall be taken in the manner desired by a majority of '. .' present, and a poll shall be granted if two electors d' . i'. Every vote tendered shall be received by the chairman unless objection be made to it. In that case the chairman shall require the person whose vote is questioned, to make the declaration required ' ' la' ' given in section 4 of this chapter). After making it, the vote must be received and recorded without further question. (School Act, secs. 46, 47 and 52.)

NOTE.—It is not competent for the chairman to reject any vote tendered. If objection be made to any vote, he should require the party to whom there is objection, to make the declaration given in section 4 of this chapter. The Inspector alone has the right, on complaint made to him, to set aside any vote given.

(3.) *Protest.*—No protest against an election, or other proceedings of the school meeting, shall be received by the chairman. All protests must be sent to the inspector, at least twenty days after the meeting. (*Ibid,* sec. 194, cl. 9.)

(4.) *Adjournment.*—A motion to adjourn an annual school meeting until the business is finished, is unlawful; but a motion to adjourn a special school meeting shall always be in order; provided that no second motion to the same effect shall be made until after some intermediate proceedings shall have been had; or provided that such special meeting has not been called for the selection of a school site. (See section 3 of chapter vii.)

(5.) *Reconsidering Motion.*—A motion to reconsider a vote may be made by any elector at the same meeting; but no vote of reconsideration shall be taken more than once on the same question at the same meeting, unless by unanimous consent.

(6.) *Close of the Meeting.*—The school meeting must not close before eleven o'clock in the forenoon, nor shall it continue open after four o'clock in the afternoon—beyond which latter hour no business can be lawfully transacted by the meeting. (School Act, secs. 39 and 41.)

(7.) *Transmitting Minutes to Inspector.*—At the close of the meeting, the chairman should sign the minutes as entered by the secretary in the minute book. Within fourteen days after the meeting, the chairman must send to the inspector a copy of the minutes (as signed by himself and the secretary), under a penalty of five dollars. (*Ibid*, sec. 50.)

(8.) *Declaration of Office.*—The trustee, or trustees elect, should at once make the declaration of office before the chairman of the meeting, or within fourteen days after the close of the meeting. In case the chairman is elected trustee, he should in like manner make the declaration of office before the secretary. (*Ibid.* sec. 19.)

NOTE.—In no case is an oath of office, or signed declaration by the trustee elect required. The act must be verbally performed. Even if it be not performed, the trustee is nevertheless a legal trustee until fined by a magistrate for neglect to make the declaration. On being fined, the office is vacated, and a new election should be at once held. Even should a trustee's election be appealed against to the inspector, the trustee himself must hold office and act until his election is legally set aside. The principle is, that an individual coming into office under colour of a legal election or appointment, is an officer *de facto* (in fact), and his acts, in relation to the public, are valid until he is lawfully removed, although it be conceded upon investigation, that his election or appointment was illegal in the first place. When his election is confirmed by the inspector, he becomes a trustee *de jure* (of right), and no further objection can be made to him, except in the rare case of an appeal against the Inspector's decision to the Minister of Education, and the reversal of that decision by him.

10.—Optional Rules.

NOTE.—The following are rules of order suggested, which may or may not be observed, at the pleasure of the meeting, viz. :—

(1.) *Addressing Chairman.*—Every elector, previous to speaking, should, unless old or infirm, rise and address himself to the chairman.

(2.) *Order of Speaking.*—When two or more electors rise at once, the chairman shall name the elector who shall speak first, when the other elector, or electors, shall next have the right to address the meeting in the order named by the chairman.

(3.) *Motion to be read.*—Each elector may require the question or motion under discussion to be read for his information at any time, but not so as to interrupt an elector who may be speaking.

(4.) *Speaking twice.*—No elector shall speak more than twice on the same question or amendment without leave of the meeting, except in explanation of something which may have been misunderstood, or until every elector choosing to speak, shall have spoken.

(5.) *Motions to be seconded.*—A motion cannot be put from the chair, or debated, unless the same be in writing (if required by the chairman), and seconded.

(6.) *Withdrawl of Motion.*—After a motion has been announced, or read by the chairman, it shall be deemed to be in the possession of the meeting ; but it may be withdrawn at any time before decision, with the consent of the meeting.

(7.) *Kinds of Motions to be received.*—When a motion is under debate, no other motion shall be received unless to amend it, or to postpone it, or for adjournment, if a special meeting, as provided in clause (4), section 9, of this chapter.

(8.) *Order of putting Motion.*—All questions shall be put in the order in which they are moved. Amendments shall always be put before the main motion : the last amendment first, and so on.

11.—First Business of the Annual School Meeting.

After appointing a chairman and secretary, the first business of the annual meeting (before electing a new trustee), is the reading of, and deciding upon, the school trustee and auditors' report for the past year. (School Act, sec. 51; for other items of business to be brought forward, see sec. 8 of this chapter.)

12.—What the Trustees' and Auditors' Report shall contain.

The law declares that the report of the trustees laid before the annual school meeting "shall (1) include a summary of their proceedings; and of the (2) state of the school during the year; together with (3) a full and detailed account of the receipt and expenditure of all school moneys received and expended on behalf of the section for any purpose whatever during the year; which report shall be signed by the trustees, and by either or both of the school auditors of the section. (Sec. 102, cl. 26.) "In case of a difference of opinion between the auditors on any matter in the account, it shall be referred to and decided by the county inspector." (*Ibid.* sec. 118, cl. 5.)

13.—Who may or may not be a Trustee.

Any fit and proper person who is a resident assessed ratepayer of the school section may be trustee thereof; but no inspector, teacher, non-resident, or supporter of a separate school can lawfully hold that office. The chairman of the meeting (if a ratepayer, and otherwise eligible) may be elected. In that case he should make a verbal declaration of office before the secretary of the meeting. (*Ibid*, secs. 37 and 226.

NOTE.—Should a person elected as trustee refuse to serve, he subjects himself to a penalty of five dollars; but a retiring trustee need not serve for four years after his term of service expires. (See chap. i., sec. 1 and 2.)

14.—Three Modes of Trustee Election prescribed.

In electing a trustee, one of the three modes authorized by custom may be adopted, viz.: (1) by acclamation; (2) by a show of hands; and (3) by polling the votes. The law requires the chairman to adopt the latter mode at the request of any two electors present, even although he may, on a show of hands, have declared the person elected. (*Ibid*, secs. 46 and 47.)

15.—School Election Complaints to be made to Inspector.

Any person having a legal objection, either to the proceedings of the annual meeting, or to the election of the trustee, has a right of appeal against either, within twenty-days, to the inspector alone. The inspector is required by law to receive and to investigate the complaint, and either confirm the proceedings and election, or set them aside, in whole or in part, within a reasonable time. (*Ibid*, sec. 194, cl. 9.)

NOTE.—Should the inspector require to examine witnesses in any election case or in regard to any other school matter, he can require them to make an affidavit or solemn affirmation before he receives their testimony. (School Act, Sec. 192.)

16.—Appeal against Decision to the Minister of Education.

Should any ratepayer object to the inspector's decision, no further proceedings should take place in the matter until an appeal is made to the head of the Education Department, and decided.

NOTE.—Should the proceedings and election be set aside, and no appeal be made to the chief superintendent within a reasonable time, the inspector, or trustees, if directed, should call another meeting for a new election. If no complaint be made to the inspector in writing within twenty days after the meeting, the proceedings (however irregular they may have been) must be held to be valid and binding upon all parties concerned. It should be borne in mind that the complaint (if made at all) must be referred, in the first place, to the inspector having jurisdiction, and not to the Minister of Education. The law provides for an appeal from the decision of the inspector in such cases to the Minister of Education. In no case should the complaint in the first instance be made to the Education Department; and, in all cases, parties appealing against an inspector's decision must send him a copy of their appeal, so that he may have an opportunity of sending an explanation to that Department.

17.—Mode of Calling Special School Meetings.

The notice calling a special school meeting should specify the place, time and objects of the meeting. It may be given by the secretary or trustees, or by the inspector. Three notices of the meeting should be put up in conspicuous places in the section, at least six days before the meeting. (School Act, sec. 102, cl. 25; see sec. 2 of this chapter.)

NOTE.—Special school meetings may be held at any convenient place in the day time, or in the evening at 7 or 8 o'clock, provided due notice be given.

18.—What an Ordinary Special School Meeting can do.

A special meeting if called to transact ordinary business, can—

(1.) *Discuss*, and decide at its pleasure, the business named in the notices calling it; or, it may (unless restricted as below)

(2.) *Adjourn* the further consideration of such business until another meeting.

(3.) *Rescind* (unless restricted as below) the resolutions of a former meeting, and pass others in their place.

19.—What a School Section Meeting cannot do.

A school meeting cannot lawfully—

(1. *Elections.*)—Rescind any resolution or vote of a former meeting for the election of a school trustee.

(2. *Contract.*)—Rescind any resolution of a former meeting, if in the meantime a contract, agreement, or other obligation has been entered into under its authority, unless at the same time it fully provides for the payment of compensation or damages caused by the rescinding of such resolution or vote.

4

(3.) *Adjourn* the annual school meeting, or any meeting called for the appointment by it and by the trustees, of arbitrators, to decide upon a school site. (See sec. 4, next chapter.)

(4. *Award*.)—Set aside or ignore the award of arbitrators appointed to select a school site.

NOTE.—By consent of the parties to the reference, an award may be reconsidered. See section 8 of the next chapter, relating to Arbitration and Awards.

(5. *Rate Bill*.)—Impose rate bill for fees, fuel, or other purposes upon residents. (See, however, chap. iv., on "Non-residents.")

(6. *Trustees' Rights*.)—Interfere with the trustees in their right to employ a teacher, erect a school house, or decide upon the expenses of the school, or the improvement of the school premises. (See note to sec. 8 of this chapter.)

CHAPTER VII.
SELECTION OF RURAL SCHOOL SITES.

1.—When a School Site requires to be chosen.

There are three cases in which the question of school site comes up for consideration in a school section : (1) on the establishment of a new section ; (2) on the change of site in an old section ; and (3) on the enlargement of an existing site.

2.—Union of Trustees and Ratepayers in choice of a Site.

Of the three cases relating to the choice of school sites which we have mentioned, the first and second only require the joint action of the trustees and ratepayers ; the third is within the province of the trustees alone to determine. (See sec. 10 of this chapter.)

3.—Meetings in regard to School Sites cannot Adjourn without action.

The necessity for joint action is clearly obvious, even without an expression of opinion when a new school section first goes into operation. It is, however, frequently difficult to determine whether the state of feeling in regard to a change of site in an old section is sufficiently decided to warrant the trustees in calling a meeting to discuss the question. However, if they know that such a feeling exists, the law requires them, within a reasonable time, to call a "special meeting" to "consider" the question. If, at this meeting, "a difference of opinion as to the site of the school" is found to exist "between the majority of the trustees and a majority of the rate-payers," the law *requires* that each party *shall* at once choose an arbitrator. It is, therefore, not competent for this special meeting to adjourn, until either the majority of the trustees and the rate-payers agree as to a site, or (in case of a difference of opinion on the subject) they respectively appoint an arbitrator to select one for them. (See next section, and sec. 8 of this chapter.)

4.—Failure to call a Meeting, or to appoint an Arbitrator.

In case the trustees refuse to call a "special meeting," as required by law, for "procuring" or "changing" a site, the inspector is authorized to do so; or, if "at such special meeting" a difference of opinion should arise in regard to a site, between the trustees and ratepayers, and the chairman, or a majority of the ratepayers by vote should unlawfully "adjourn the meeting," (and thus neglect or refuse to appoint an arbitrator,) the law declares that then "it shall be competent for the county inspector, with the arbitrator appointed, to meet and determine the matter; and the inspector, in case of such refusal and neglect, shall have a second or casting vote, provided" that he and the one arbitrator appointed "should not agree." (School Act, secs. 121 and 124.)

5.—Remedy in case an Arbitrator should refuse to Act.

"Should only a majority of the arbitrators appointed" to select a site, "be present at any lawful meeting, in consequence of the neglect or the refusal of their colleague to meet them, it shall be competent for the arbitrators present to make and publish an award upon the matter submitted to them, or to adjourn the meeting for any period not exceeding ten days, and give the absent arbitrator notice of such adjournment." (*Ibid,* sec. 125.)

6.—Power of the Arbitrators.—Kind of Site to be chosen.

The law says, that "in case of a difference as to the choice of a site," the arbitrators appointed "or a majority of them present at any lawful meeting shall have authority to make and publish an award upon the matter or matters submitted to them." Unless, therefore, the choice of one out of two or more sites in dispute is the matter submitted to them, their choice of any site in the section is left free, and they should choose one best adapted to the wants of the section. It should be an acre in size (but cannot be less than half an acre), in a pleasant situation, and (without the consent of the *owner* of the site chosen) should not be within a hundred yards of *his* house, orchard, pleasure-ground or dwelling-house, although it may be close up to the orchard and dwelling-house of any other party. (*Ibid.* secs. 121 and 123.)

NOTE.—Arbitrators are "entitled to the same remuneration *per diem* for the time employed" as are county councillors; "and the parties concerned shall pay all the expenses of the arbitration," according to the award of the arbitrators. (*Ibid,* sec. 127.)

7.—Making and Publishing a written or parol Award.

When the arbitrators have agreed upon their award, they should reduce it to writing, sign and seal it. This is "making" the award. When thus made, it should be sent to the trustees, for their information and that of the ratepayers. This is "publishing" it. It is competent, however, for the arbitrators to declare or publish the award orally, in presence of the parties concerned, viz., a public meeting of the trustees and ratepayers. Should the award thus published be afterwards, by consent, reduced to writing (as above), it should be identical in its terms with the oral declaration made, that is, it should be merely a written record of it. Any material variation in the written record of the oral award would destroy its validity and finality. (See *Davis* v. *McGivern.* 11 Q. B. R. 112.)

NOTE.—An award may, with the consent, or at the request, of the parties to the reference, be reconsidered. (See sec. 9 of this chapter.)

8.—Summary of General Rules in Regard to Arbitrations.

NOTE.—The following are some of the general regulations which govern arbitrations. They are inserted for the guidance and information of the arbitrators.

(1.) *Constitution of the Arbitration Court.*—Any one who can contract, can submit matters in dispute to arbitration. Either a friend or enemy, or a person having an interest in the cause, may be chosen.[*] Persons unimpeachable on the score of interest or capacity should, if possible, be chosen, and no arbitrator should act as the partisan of the persons appointing him. He should divest himself of all prejudice. If an arbitrator acts corruptly, or with manifest partiality, or colludes with one of the parties, the award is bad. All the arbitrators should be chosen before proceeding to the arbitration, except where otherwise provided (as in the case of a school site.) Notification in writing to the person chosen, and acceptance by him of the office, are necessary, to complete the appointment. Where there are an odd number of arbitrators, a majority decides all matters submitted to them, but where the number appointed is two, four, &c., who are equally divided in their opinions, any person who may be selected as umpire has the sole right to determine the points of difference, and make the award. The inspector is, *ex officio* and virtually, umpire in cases where he and another arbitrator only are present, as he has, in the absence of one of his co-arbitrators, a second or casting vote. In arbitrations under the School Law the directions of the statute should be strictly complied with. Reasonable notice of a meeting must be given to each arbitrator. If one or more be absent, the meeting should be adjourned for about ten days, and notice of another meeting again sent to each arbitrator. At the subsequent meeting, duly notified, two arbitrators can act without their colleague, and make and publish an award.

(2.) *Duties of Arbitrators.*—It is the duty of arbitrators to hear evidence on both sides; one witness may be excluded while the other is being examined. They are the judges of the *admissibility* of evidence, so far as the competency of the witness is concerned, as well as of the law and facts of the case. If parties to the arbitration and their witnesses, who are duly notified, or who know of the arbitration, do not attend, the arbitrators can proceed *ex parte*, and decide according to the best evidence before them. Where evidence is received, however, it should always be taken in the presence of the parties to the reference, or some

---

[*] The principle laid down in the Municipal Act should, if possible, be acted upon, viz.: "No member, officer or person in the employ, &c., of any corporation which is concerned or interested in the arbitration * * * shall be appointed to act as an arbitrator in any case of of arbitration under this Act." (Sec. 376.)

one attending on their behalf. Before closing, the arbitrators should receive all the evidence tendered on both sides, and should takes notes of it. An arbitrator cannot delegate his power; but, if he obtains the opinion of professional men, he may adopt it as his own. He may, however, delegate purely ministerial acts, such as to go from one place to another, to obtain certain definite information, or estimate the value of some specific work performed; but he cannot direct any person to commit a trespass.

(3.) *Time of making an award.*—If no time be fixed, an award should be made and published within three months from the time of the submission. The time for making an award may, however, be enlarged by the parties to the submission. If time lapses, the power of the arbitrators is gone until it is enlarged.

(4.) *Making and publishing an award.*—If the award be in writing, (as, under the Municipal Law, (Sec. 290) it must be,) it should be signed in the presence of an attesting witness. Where there are two or more arbitrators, all (or the majority, if all be not present) must execute the award at the same time and place, and in the presence of each other, and an opportunity should be given to the minority (if disposed) to join or not in the award. An award, however, may be made and published orally. An award is made when the arbitrators have signed it. When so signed by the arbitrators and witnessed, their power is gone, and no single arbitrator can remedy a mistake or correct a blunder. It must be done by the signers, and with the consent of the parties to the reference. An award is published when it is sent to either or both of the parties concerned, or notice is sent to them that it is ready to be delivered. It should be delivered on the day fixed, and then the fees and other expenses on it are payable. Any kind of words may be used in an award; but they should be definite, conclusive and final on all the points submitted. Arbitrators are not required to give reasons for their award, nor are they answerable for want of skill in performing their duties; but an arbitrator may be called as a witness to prove *facts* which occurred or came under his notice during the reference.

(5.) *Judgment and Experience.*—In *Martin* v. *Kergan* (2 Prac. R. 370), it was held that the parties to an arbitration "have a right to the arguments, experience and judgment of each arbitrator, at every stage of the proceedings."

(6.) *Costs of Arbitration.*—Where the costs of the arbitration are at the discretion of the arbitrators, and the award says nothing about them, each party pays his own costs of reference, and the costs of the award are to be borne equally. (*Glen* v. *Grand Trunk Railway*, 2 Prac. R. 377.) Under the School Law the costs may be fixed at the discretion of the arbitrators. The award need not be given up until the amount of costs thus avoided be paid.

(7.) *When an award is bad.*—(1) When it is uncertain and not final. (2) When it contains a mistake on the face of it. (3) When the proceedings are irregular, as want of notice of meetings, improper conduct of arbitrators in receiving evidence. (4) Corruption or collusion on the part of the arbitrators. (5) Fraud or concealment of material evidence. (6) When the award cannot be acted upon.

(8.) *Arbitration, before award made, may be superseded by mutual concurrence.*—Chief Justice Robinson thus laid down the law on this subject:—As a general rule, we take it that where two parties have a difference upon any matter of business, and refer it to arbitration, they may afterwards agree upon the matter on which they had differed, and so may render it unnecessary that any award should be made. By the common law either party might, before the award made, revoke the submission.—There have been restrictions lately placed by statute upon this right of one party to revoke without the concurrence of the other, but it would be most unreasonable and inconvenient to hold that both the parties may not come to

a settlement of their dispute, and so dispense with the necessity for the arbitrators proceeding.—*Chief Justice Robinson, in re Vance* v. *King et al, No. 1, Hallowell.* 21 Q. B. R. 187.

(9.) An award in regard to the selection of a school site may be reconsidered.
(See the next section of this chapter.)

9.—Power of School Meetings in regard to "Awards."

Even after an arbitrator or arbitrators have been appointed to
select a site, it is competent for a majority of the trustees and of a
public school meeting called for that purpose to agree upon the choice
of a site before an award is made. Such an agreement revokes the
submission of the matter to arbitrators, who should at once be notified
of the fact, so that no award may be "made." The School law provides an easy way of meeting the difficulty, should an award be made
which is not satisfactory. It provides that "with the consent, or at
the request of the parties to the reference, the arbitrators, or a majority of them, shall have authority, within three months from the
date of their award, to reconsider such award, and make and publish
a second award, which award (or the previous one, if not reconsidered
by the arbitrators) shall be binding upon all parties concerned, for at
least one year from the date thereof." (School Act, sec. 122.)

10.—Power of the Trustees in Enlarging a School Site.

Where no desire is felt by the trustees or ratepayers to change the
site of a section, the trustees have full power to enlarge it at their
discretion to an acre or more in extent, and to erect a new school
house on it, or to repair or enlarge the old one, without consulting
their constituents. (See secs. 2 and 13 of this chapter.)

11.—Sale or Exchange of the old School Site.

Trustees are required "to dispose by sale or otherwise, of any
school site or school property not required by them, in consequence
of a change of school site, or other cause, and to convey the same
under their corporate seal, and to apply the proceeds thereof for their
lawful school purposes." (School Act, sec. 102, cl. 7.)

NOTE.—This case differs materially from one in which a change of boundaries
necessitates a change of site. Under such circumstances the law declares that,
"In case a school site or school house or other school property *be no longer
required*[*] in a section, in consequence of the alteration or the union of school sections, the same shall be disposed of by sale or otherwise, in such manner as a
majority of the assessed freeholders and householders in the altered or united
school sections may decide at a public meeting called for that purpose." "The
inhabitants transferred from one school section to another shall be entitled, for the
public school purposes of the section to which they are attached, to such a
proportion of the proceeds of the sale of such school house or other public school
property, [after, of course, paying the debts of the section,] as the assessed value
of their property bears to that of the other inhabitants of the school section from
which they have been so separated." The residue of such proceeds shall be
applied to the erection of a new school house in the old school section, or to other
public school purposes of such old school section." In the case of united sections,
the proceeds of the sale shall be applied to the like public school purposes of such
united sections. (*Ibid*, sec. 86.)

* A full explanation of the phrase "no longer required" here used, will be found in Part II.
of these Lectures, chap. iii, sec. 11.

12.—Owner of Land must Sell School Sites selected.

If the owner of a newly selected school site, or of land adjoining an old site (which the trustees have decided to 'enlarge), should refuse to sell it, or should ask an unreasonable price for it, the law requires the trustees and owners each to appoint an arbitrator to appraise the damages, to the owner, of such compulsory sale. Upon the tender of payment of these damages to the owner of the land by the trustees, they can take possession of the land for school purposes, and proceed to erect a school house on it, or to enclose it. (*Ibid*, sec. 123.)

13.—Privileges of the Owner only relate to a New Site.

On the selection of a person's land for a new school site (with or without his knowledge), within one hundred yards of his garden, orchard, pleasure-ground, or dwelling house, the owner may either consent to the sale of the new site at a reasonable rate, or he may refuse to sell it, at his pleasure; but he cannot be compelled to sell it. In regard to the *enlargement* of the old school site, however, the law gives the owner of the chosen land only a restricted privilege, should the trustees offer to buy it. But they can compel a sale when the proposed enlargement is not "made in the *direction* of the orchard, garden, or dwelling-house," provided that it cannot be otherwise enlarged. Without the consent of the owner no part of the garden or grounds attached to the house can be taken. In case of refusal to sell it (within these restrictions), the law requires the trustees and owner, each, to appoint an arbitrator to appraise the damages, and upon tender by the trustees (as above) of the amount of damages awarded, the trustees can take possession and use the land for the purposes of their trust. (*Ibid*, sec. 123.)

NOTE.—The provisions of the law on the compulsory sale of school sites are twofold, although they have been frequently confounded together. Clauses 1 and 4 of the 123rd section refer 1st to "the selection of land" "for a rural *school site*," and clauses 5 and 6 to the selection of land for *enlarging existing school premises*. In these two cases, the trustees can demand an arbitration should the owner of the selected or enlarged site refuse to sell, or ask too large a price for the land. In the first class of cases, (*i.e.*, the selection of a *new* site,) the owner can lawfully refuse to sell, or to submit to arbitration, when the site selected is within 100 yards of *his* "orchard, garden, pleasure ground or dwelling-house;" but where the trustees merely wish to enlarge their existing school premises, the owner has only a restricted right, (as explained above,) which shall not "be held to restrict trustees in the enlargement of a school site, existing [on the 24th of March, 1874], to the required dimensions." (Sec. 123.) The provision of the law does not in any case (as has been supposed) apply to other persons whose house, orchard, &c., may happen to be within 100 yards of the proposed site, and who are not in any way concerned in the sale of land for the enlarged site.

14.—Township Councils may Purchase School Sites.

The Municipal Institutions Act authorizes township councils to pass by-laws "for obtaining such real property as may be required for the erection of public school houses thereon, and for other public school purposes, and for the disposal thereof when no longer required; and for providing for the establishment and support of public schools according to law." (Sec. 461, cl. 6.)

NOTE.—The latter part of this section would imply that it is not in the power of township councils to apply clergy reserve or other township moneys to the establishment or support of schools, except as according to law, (i.e., the school law,) and that is on the principle of the average attendance of pupils. (See decision of the Courts on this point in Part II of these Lectures, chapter ix. sec. 5.)

15.—Decisions of the Courts in regard to School Sites.

(1.) *In selecting a Site, Trustees cannot act without consulting their constituents.* —The Court of Queen's Bench has decided that the trustees cannot, without reference to the [assessed] freeholders and householders of the section, determine upon a site for the school house, and impose a rate to meet the expense of its purchase.—*Orr* v. *Ranney et al, No. 15, Westminster.* 12 Q. B. R. 377.

(2.) *Arbitration before award made may be superseded by mutual concurrence.*— Chief Justice Robinson thus laid down the law on this subject:—As a general rule, we take it that where two parties have a difference upon any matter of business, and refer it to arbitration, they may afterwards agree upon the matter on which they had differed, and so may render it unnecessary that any award should be made. By the common law either party might, before the award made, revoke the submission. There have been restrictions lately placed by statute upon this right of one party to revoke without the concurrence of the other, but it would be most unreasonable and inconvenient to hold that both the parties may not come to a settlement of their dispute, and so dispense with the necessity for the arbitrators proceeding.—*Chief Justice Robinson, in re Vance* v. *King et al, No. 1, Hallowell.* 22 Q. B. R. 187.

(3.) *First arbitration in regard to a School Site cannot be set aside by a subsequent Special Meeting.*—The Court of Common Pleas has decided the following case: When a meeting was held to change the site of a school house, and arbitrators appointed, who met and decided the question, but their decision was not acted upon; subsequently another meeting was called, and their decision and proceedings were acted upon and the site changed. *Held,* that the proceedings were irregular, and that the trustees had no authority to change the site of the school house without the sanction of a special meeting of the [assessed] freeholders and householders, and that the second meeting had no authority to alter the determinations previously made.—*Williams* v. *Trustees, No. 8, Plympton.* 7 C. P. R. 559.

(4.) *Replevin—Arbitration in regard to School Site—Blanks filled in after execution—Award rendered invalid thereby* —The Court of Common Pleas decided the following case: *Replevin.*[*]—Two defendants avowed [i.e., maintained and justified the act done by them]; the third pleaded the convening of a special meeting of freeholders and householders of a certain school section to procure a school site, when it was agreed to procure a certain piece of ground and erect a school house thereon, which was done. That plaintiff was a resident freeholder when the meeting was held and when his goods were seized, and was assessed $80 for building said school, &c. The plaintiff pleaded that the meeting above set forth was null and void, because before the said meeting another had been convened according to law, when a difference of opinion existed between a majority of the freeholders and householders as to choosing a school site, and arbitrators were appointed, who decided upon a certain site, which decision remains in force, and the defendants in contravention thereof wrongfully purchased the site mentioned in

---

[*] *Replevin:* the name of an action for the recovery of goods and chattels. *Replevy:* to re-deliver goods which have been distrained, to the original possessor of them, on his giving pledges in an action of replevin.

their plea, and wrongfully distrained, &c.   Upon demurrer, *Held*, that the second meeting pleaded by the defendant was a violation of the provisions of the statute, and that the plaintiff was entitled to judgment.   The arbitrators to whom a reference in this cause was made under the School Act, executed an award, the description of the lot not being fully inserted, but a blank being left therefor, which was afterwards filled in and the word lot altered into gore.   *Held*, that the award was insufficient.   *Held*, also, that school trustees who executed a warrant as such trustees under the seal of the trustee corporation, were not personally responsible. —*Ryland* v. *King et al, No. 1, Hallowell.* [See decision of the Queen's Bench below, in effect reversing this case.] 12 C. P. R. 198.   For definition of the word "*replevin*" see * below.

(5.) *A similar case decided by the Court of Queen's Bench.*—Replevin against two school trustees and one King, a bailiff, for a horse.   Defendants pleaded, 1, That they did not take ; and 2, an avowry, setting out in substance that on the 30th of October, 1858, a special meeting of the freeholders and householders of the section had been duly called to procure a school site and erect a school house thereon, at which it was agreed to procure a certain site named : that this was procured and the school house built: that the plaintiff was duly assessed for a sum specified : that the trustees by their warrant commanded King to collect it ; and that after demand and default made he seized the horse.   The plaintiff pleaded to the avowry, 1st, *de injuriâ;* and, 2nd, as to the justification by the trustees, that the meeting was void, because before it took place a special meeting of the freeholders was duly held to procure a school site, at which a majority of the trustees differed from a majority of those present with regard to the site, in consequence of which the freeholders and householders, the trustees and local superintendent, each appointed an arbitrator to decide the question ; that the arbitrators determined upon a site specified, different from that mentioned in the avowry, which award remained in force ; and that the trustees, contrary to this decision, wrongfully purchased the site mentioned in the avowry.   The defendants replied that there was no such award.   As to this issue taken upon the first plea of the defendants, it appeared that the horse was seized by King under a warrant signed by two trustees, commencing: "We, the undersigned trustees of school section," &c., and sealed with the corporate seal.   *Held*, that the trustees were liable personally, not in their corporate capacities only.   With regard to the second and third issues, raised by the plea of *de injuriâ* to the avowry, and replication denying the award, the evidence showed that in 1857 the inhabitants were divided as to the choice of a school site, and an award was made but not acted upon: that in 1858 the same difference existed, and one of the trustees also differed from his co-trustees; that in March the two trustees, defendants, obtained a conveyance of half an acre, part of lot 15, and in May a meeting was held at which arbitrators were named and an award made ; but the inhabitants being still dissatisfied, another meeting was held in July, when the arbitrators mentioned in the plea to the avowry were chosen.   In the meantime the building was commenced upon the land conveyed.   On the 4th of September an award was drawn up [in which a blank was left for a description of the site].   On the 30th of October, 1858, a meeting was held, having been regularly called by the two trustees, to settle the question finally, and a resolution passed adopting [as the site] the land conveyed.   In April, 1859, the two trustees, defendants, met, the third being absent from the country, and resolved upon the rate, which was inserted by the clerk in the roll, and the warrant was issued to King, who seized the plaintiff's horse.   The plaintiff, after that, set about getting the award of September, 1858, which was afterwards filled up by two of the arbitrators, who stated that it had been left blank because they did not know the precise description of London's land.   *Held*, that upon the second issue raised by plaintiff, defendants were entitled to succeed, for the evidence sustained the avowry.   And that upon the third issue r..ised by the plaintiff they were also entitled to the verdict, for there was in fact no award made, and even as it was altered after execution the description was too uncertain.   Ryland v. The same defendants, in the Court of Common

Pleas, commented upon. [See above.] *Held,* that under the circumstances proved, the reference did not make the subsequent meeting illegal. *Held,* also, upon demurrer, that the avowry was good, the omission of any averment essential to the validity of the fate being cured by the second plea of the plaintiff to it, which relied wholly upon the award: that the second plea of the plaintiff was bad, for not showing that before the award the trustees and inhabitants had not duly selected the site built upon, as they might do notwithstanding the reference; and that the replication to it denying the award was a good answer. *Vance* v. *King et al, No. 1, Hallowell.* 21 Q. B. R. 187.

NOTE.—See also decisions of the Superior Courts in regard to School Houses, chapter ii, section 13, pages 21 and 22.

CHAPTER VIII.

COMPULSORY ATTENDANCE OF ABSENTEE CHILDREN.

1.—Right of every Child to receive an Education.

The public school law declares that "every child, from the age of seven to twelve years inclusive, shall have the right to attend some school, or be otherwise educated, for four months in every year; * and any parent or guardian who does not provide that every child between those ages under his care shall attend some school, or be otherwise educated, as thus of right declared, shall be subject to the penalties provided by this Act." (Sec. 8.)

NOTE.—This provision of the Act does not require any Roman Catholic to attend a public school, or a Protestant to attend a Roman Catholic separate school.

2.—Duty of School Trustees in this matter.

The law makes it also the duty of the trustees of every public school:—

(1.) "To ascertain before the thirty-first day of December in every year, through the assessor, collector or some other person to be appointed for that purpose, and paid by them, the names, ages and residences of all the children of school age in their school section, distinguishing those children (between the ages of seven and twelve years) who have not attended any school (or who have not been otherwise educated) for four months of the year. (Sec. 210.)

---

* While the school law thus declares the right of every child to attend school and receive an education therein, *(or otherwise)* it also very properly makes it the imperative *duty* of trustees to provide in their school house sufficient "accommodation" or room for the attendance of every child of school age in the section, at the rate of nine square feet of space on the floor for each child. (See chap. ii, sec. 9, page 19.)

* The form to be used by trustees in taking the school census will be furnished by Messrs. Copp, Clark & Co., Toronto, free by post for 5 cts.

(2.) "To notify personally, or by letter or otherwise, the parents or guardians of such children of the neglect or violation on their part of the provisions of the law on this subject.—*Ibid.*

(3.) "In case, after having been so notified, the parents or guardians of such children continue to neglect or violate the provisions of this Act, it shall be the duty of the trustees to impose a rate-bill on such parents or guardians not exceeding one dollar per month for each of their children not attending school; or,

(4.) "To make complaint of such neglect or violation to a magistrate having jurisdiction in such cases, unless they are satisfied that such neglect or violation has not been wilful, or caused by poverty, ill-health, or too great distance from school."

3.—Power and Duty of the Police or other Magistrate.

The school law also declares that: "It shall be competent for the police magistrate of any city or town, and for any magistrate in any village, township or town where there is no police magistrate, to investigate and decide upon any complaint made by the trustees, or any person authorized by them, against any parent or guardian for the violation of the next preceding sections of this Act [which declare the right of children to attend school; (see sec. 1 of this chapter,)] and to impose a fine not exceeding *five* dollars for the first wilful offence, and double that penalty for every subsequent offence; which fine and penalty shall be enforced as are other fines in the School Act." (Sec. 211.)

(a) "The police magistrate or justice shall not be bound to, but may, in his discretion, forego to issue the warrant for the imprisonment of the offender, as in said section is provided."—*Ibid.*

(b) "It shall be the duty of the police magistrate, or any magistrate where there is no police magistrate, to ascertain, as far as may be, the circumstances of any party complained of for not sending his child or children to some school, or otherwise educating him or them, and whether the alleged violation has been wilful, or has been caused by extreme poverty, or ill-health, or too great a distance from any school; and in any of the latter cases, the magistrate shall not award punishment, but shall report the circumstances to the trustees of the school section or division in which the offence has occurred." (Sec. 212).

NOTE.—It will be seen from these sections of the Act that school trustees are made responsible for carrying out the "compulsory" sections of the Act quoted. Should they neglect to impose the required rate bill, as provided, or to duly report every case of delinquency to the magistrate, they become personally responsible for the amount of the rate bill or of the fine which may be lost to the section or division in consequence of such neglect on their part. Besides, they are responsible for the loss of the apportionment which would have been made on the average attendance of the absentees.

CHAPTER IX.

PUBLIC SCHOOL TEACHERS.

1.—Who are qualified Public School Teachers.

A duly qualified public school teacher is one who, at the time of engaging with the trustees, and during the whole time of teaching their school, is possessed of a "legal certificate of qualification" (whether first, second or third class), issued under the authority of the Consolidated Public School Act of Ontario. (Sec. 162.)

NOTE.—The law expressly declares that every person receiving any part of the school fund (as teacher or assistant) shall hold a legal certificate of qualification. The Superior Courts have also decided that trustees cannot legally levy a rate for the payment of a teacher who does not possess the necessary qualifications as such, under the school laws. (See clause 4, sec. 12 of this chap.)

2.—Who cannot hold the office of Public School Teacher.

No high, or public school trustee, and no inspector, can lawfully hold the office of, or act as, a public school teacher, and *vice versa*. (School Act, sec. 226.)

NOTE.—For conditions on which teachers may obtain certificates of qualification, see chapter xiv.

3.—Assistant Teachers in a Public School.

Whenever the number of pupils enrolled in a public school exceeds *fifty*, the trustees are required to "employ an additional teacher as an assistant." A monitor cannot take the place of an "assistant teacher," or be put in charge of a division of the school. He can only aid the master or assistant in the classes.

NOTE.—Certificates may be granted by inspectors to assistant teachers and monitors for a year; subject to renewal. (See chap. xiv.)

4.—Agreements between Trustees and Teachers.

"All agreements between trustees and teachers, to be valid and binding, shall be in writing, signed by the parties thereto, and sealed with the corporate seal of the trustees," and "may lawfully include any stipulation to provide the teacher with board and lodging." (School Act, sec. 161.) Payment may also be made quarterly.

NOTE.—All agreements between trustees and a teacher, to be valid, must be authorized at a regular or special meeting of the trustees, and must be signed by at least two of the trustees and a teacher; they must also have the *corporate seal* of the section attached to them (as above), otherwise the trustees may be made *personally responsible* for the fulfilment of such agreements, and can then be sued on them individually by the teacher. It should also be entered in the trustees' book, and a copy of it given to the teacher.* The trustees being a corporation, their agreement with their teacher is binding on their successors in office, if made in accordance with the foregoing section; and should they refuse or wilfully neglect to exercise the corporate powers vested in them to give it effect, they would be personally liable for the amount due a teacher. The mode of settling disputes between trustees and a teacher is by suit in the Division Court. (Public School Law, secs. 161, 165, and 238.

NOTE.—See "Decisions of the Courts relating to Trustees and Teachers," section 10 of this chapter.

5.—General powers of the Master of a Public School.

In every school in which there are two or more teachers employed therein, the trustees shall determine who shall be considered as the master of the school.

NOTE.—The head teacher employed in any public school in which there is more than one teacher, shall be designated and known as the *master;* and the others shall be named first, second or third, &c., assistant *teacher*.

The master of every school is a public officer, and, as such, shall have power, and it shall be his duty to observe and enforce the following rules:—

(1.) *See that the Rules are observed.*—He shall see that the general rules and regulations, and any special rules (not inconsistent with them) which may be approved by the trustees for their respective schools, are duly and faithfully carried out, subject to appeal, in case of dissatisfaction, to the inspector.

NOTE.—The master is required to read, or cause to be read, in his school, at least once in each quarter, (or otherwise inform the pupils of,) so much of the regulations as shall be necessary to give them a proper understanding of the rules by which they are governed.

(2.) *Prescribed Duties of Teachers.*—He shall prescribe (with the assent of the trustees) the duties of the several teachers in his school, but he shall be responsible for the control and management of the classes under their charge.

(3.) *Religious Exercises—Ten Commandments.*—He shall see that the regulations in regard to *Opening and Closing Exercises of the Day* are observed, and that the Ten Commandments are duly taught to all the pupils, and repeated by them once a week.

6.—Discipline in the School—Authority over Pupils.

It shall also be the duty of each master and teacher of a public school, to observe the following regulations:—

(1.) *General Principles of Government.*—Masters and teachers are to evince a regard for the improvement and general welfare of their pupils; treat them with kindness, combined with firmness, and aim

* Forms of agreement between trustees and teacher, can be obtained from Messrs. Copp, Clark & Co., free by post, for 5 cents.

at governing them by their affections and reason, rather than by harshness and severity. Teachers shall also, as far as practicable, exercise a general care over their pupils in and out of school, and shall not confine their instructions and superintendence to the usual school duties, but shall, as far as possible, extend the same to the mental and moral training of such pupils, to their personal deportment, to the practice of correct habits and good manners among them, and to omit no opportunity of inculcating the principles of TRUTH and HONESTY, the duties of respect to superiors, and obedience to all persons placed in authority over them.

(2.) *Discipline.*—Each master and teacher shall practice such discipline in his school class or department, as would be exercised by a kind, firm and judicious parent in his family. It is strictly enjoined upon all teachers in the schools to avoid the appearance of indiscreet haste in the discipline of their pupils; and in any difficult cases which may occur, to apply to the master, [if an assistant,] inspector, or to the trustees, (as the case may be,) for advice and direction.

NOTE.—The following are modes to be adopted or avoided:—

(1.) *Proper.*—Reproof, kindly but firmly given, either in private or before the school, as circumstances require it, or such severe punishment as the case really warrants, administered as directed in the above regulation.

(2.) *Improper.*—Contemptuous language, reproof administered in passion, personal indignity or torture, and violation of the laws of health.

(3.) *State of feeling among Pupils.*—Masters and teachers shall cultivate kindly and affectionate feelings among the pupils; discountenance quarrelling, cruelty to animals, and every approach to vice.

(4.) *Power to suspend Pupils.*—The master shall suspend (subject to appeal, by the parent or guardian, to the trustees) any pupil for any of the following reasons:—

   (a) Truancy persisted in.
   (b) Violent opposition to authority.
   (c) Repetition of any offence after notice.
   (d) Habitual and determined neglect of duty.
   (e) The use of profane, or other improper language.
   (f) General bad conduct, and bad example, to the injury of the school.

(5.) Cutting, marring, destroying, defacing or injuring any of the public school property, such as buildings, furniture, seats, fences, trees, shrubbery, &c., or writing any obscene or improper words on the fences, walls, privies, or any part of the premises, provided that any master suspending a pupil for any of the causes above named, shall, immediately after such suspension, give notice thereof, in writing, to the parent or guardian of such pupil, and to the trustees, in which notice shall be stated the reason for such suspension; but no pupil shall be expelled without the authority of the trustees.

(6.) *Expulsion of Pupils.*—When the example of any pupil is very hurtful to the school, and in all cases where reformation appears hopeless, it shall be the duty of the master, with the approbation of the trustees, to expel such pupil from the school.   But any pupil under public censure, who shall express to the master his regret for such a course of conduct, as openly and explicitly as the case may require, shall, with the approbation of the trustees and master, be re-admitted to the school.

NOTE.—The School Law declares that "any pupil who shall be adjudged so refractory by the trustees (or a majority of them) and the teacher, that his presence in school is deemed injurious to the other pupils, may be dismissed from such school, and, where practicable, removed to an Industrial school."(Sec. 102, cl. 22.)

NOTE.—The master, under clause (2) of section 5 of this chapter, may authorize the assistant to suspend or otherwise deal with pupils in his class, as provided in clause (4) of this section.

7.—Duties of Masters and Teachers in regard to Teaching.

The law requires each master or teacher of a public school:

(1.) "*To Teach Diligently* and faithfully all the branches required to be taught in the school, according to the terms of his engagement with the trustees, and according to the provisions of the School Act, and the authorized regulations under it."   (School Act, sec. 163.)

(2.) *Classify Pupils.*—He shall classify the children according to the books used; study those books himself, and teach according to the improved method recommended in their prefaces.   The division of the pupils into classes, as prescribed by the programme, shall be strictly observed; and no teacher shall be allowed to take his or her class beyond the limits fixed for the classes taught by such teachers, without the consent of the master (if an assistant) or inspector, except for occasional reviews; but individual pupils, on being quali-fied, may, with the consent of the master, be advanced from a lower to the higher class.

(3.) *Constant employment to Pupils.*—He shall give the children under his charge constant employment in the studies prescribed in the authorized programme; and endeavour by judicious and diversified modes, to render the exercises of the school pleasant as well as profitable.   In giving out the lessons for the next day, difficult parts should be explained, and where necessary, the best mode of studying them should be pointed out to the pupils.

NOTE.—The object of the school programme is two-fold—to provide work, (1), for the master or teacher, and (2), for the pupils while he is engaged.   No master is required to teach more than 27½ hours per week; but while he is teaching one class one subject, the other classes should be engaged in studying the other subjects, according to the programme.

(4.) *Time-Table.*—Each master shall keep, in some conspicuous place in the school-room, a time-table, showing the order of exercises for each day in the week, and the time for each exercise, as prescribed in the programme of studies for public schools.

(5.) *Merit Cards—Prizes.*—In all the schools the series of merit cards, prepared and authorized by the Education Department, shall be regularly used; and if prizes are given, it must be on the principles laid down in the explanatory memorandum accompanying that series of cards.

(6.) *Quarterly Examination.*—Each class in every school shall be open for public examination and inspection during the last week of every quarter; and the master or teacher shall call upon every pupil in the school, unless excused, to review or recite in the course of such examination.

NOTE.—See clause (1) of section 13, of this chapter.

(7.) *In School at* 8¾ *a.m., &c.*—All teachers shall be in their respective schools, and open their rooms for the reception of pupils, at least fifteen minutes in the morning and five minutes in the afternoon before the specified time for beginning school; and during school hours they shall faithfully devote themselves to the duties of their office.

8.—Duties of Teachers in regard to School Premises.

(1.) *Care of School Property.*—Each master [or teacher] shall exercise the strictest vigilance over the public school property in his charge—the building, outhouses, fences, &c., furniture, apparatus, and books belonging to the school, so that they may receive no injury; and give prompt notice, in writing, to the trustees or person appointed by them, under section 12, chapter ii, (if in cities, towns or villages, to the inspector,) of any repairs which may require to be made to the building, premises, or furniture, &c., and of any furniture or supplies which may be required for the school.

(2.) *Regulations in regard to School Premises, &c.*—The trustees having made such provision relative to the school house and its appendages as required by law (see section 9, chapter ii), it shall be the duty of the master to give strict attention to the proper ventilation and temperature, as well as to the cleanliness of the school house; he shall also prescribe such rules for the use of the yard and out-buildings connected with the school house as will insure their being kept in a neat and proper condition; and he shall be held responsible for any want of cleanliness about the premises.

(3.) *School open for Pupils.*—Care must be taken to have the school house ready for the reception of pupils at least *fifteen* minutes before the time prescribed for opening the school, in order to afford shelter to those who may arrive before the appointed hour. (See clause (7), section 7 of this chapter.)

(4.) *Out-Premises.*—The master [or teacher] shall see that the yards, sheds, privies, and other out-buildings are kept in order, and that the school house and buildings are looked at all proper times; and that all deposits of sweepings from rooms or yards are removed from the premises.

(5.) *Fires and Sweeping.*—He shall employ, at a compensation to be fixed by the trustees, a suitable person to make fires, to sweep the rooms and halls daily, and dust the windows, walls, seats, desks, and other furniture in the same; but no master, assistant teacher, or pupil shall be required to perform such duty, unless voluntarily, and with suitable compensation.

9.—Duties of Teachers in regard to Library, Reports, &c.

(1.) *Act as Librarian.*—Each master [or teacher] shall act as librarian of the school, and take charge of the books; also make, keep, and preserve a catalogue of the same; deliver, charge, receive, and credit the volumes given out, and keep a register of the same; number, label, and catalogue the books; and make returns of the library, its books, &c., as required by the library regulations.

(2.) *The Library.*—He shall keep the library open for the distribution (and return) of books to the scholars and ratepayers of the school division, on Friday afternoon of each week; but this duty shall not be permitted to interfere with the regular exercises of the school.

(3.) *General Register.*—He shall keep a general register of the school (to be furnished at the expense of the trustees), in which shall be entered, in each term, the date of the admission of each pupil; the names of the pupils in each of the classes in the school; the promotion of pupils; date of a pupil's leaving the school, and destination, both as to place and occupation; and such other information as shall at all times give a correct idea of the condition of the school.

(4.) *Daily Register.*—He shall also keep the daily register (provided at the expense of the trustees), in which shall be entered the names and daily attendance of pupils, their proficiency in various studies, and other information.

NOTE.—See clause (3), of section 13 of this chapter.

(5.) *Returns.*—The master [or teacher] shall make such returns, and at such times, as may be required by the [master] inspector, or trustees, relating to his class, school, or department.

(6.) *Reports.*—He shall make the necessary term special, or annual reports to, and with, the trustees, to the inspector or chief superintendent, at such times and in such manner as may be required.

NOTE.—See section 21 of chapter ii, (page 24), and clause (4) of section 13 of this chapter.

5

10.—Regulations in regard to Sickness, Visiting Schools, Visitors, Presents, Teachers' Meetings, &c.

(1.) *Absence and Sickness.*—No master or teacher shall be absent from the school in which he or she may be employed, without permission of the trustees or inspector, except in case of sickness, in which case the absence of such teacher shall be immediately reported to the trustees; and no deduction from the salary of a teacher shall be made on account of sickness, (not exceeding at the rate of four weeks for the whole year,) as certified by a medical man. (High School Act, sec. 51.)

NOTE.—See latter part of section 15, of this chapter.

(2.) *Visiting Schools.*—The inspector may permit a public school master, or teacher, to be absent two of the ordinary teaching days in each half year, for the purpose of visiting and observing the methods of classification, teaching, and discipline practised in other schools than that in which he or she teaches.

NOTE.—This visit, with the name of the school or schools visited, is to be duly reported by such master or teacher to the inspector. Each public school master and teacher must give at least three days' notice of each visit to the trustees. In order that no loss of apportionment may accrue to any school in consequence of the master's absence under this regulation, a proportionate amount of average attendance will be credited to the school for the time so employed by the teacher; but under no circumstances can lost time be lawfully made up by teaching on any of the prescribed vacations, holidays, or half holidays, nor will time be allowed by the Department, or be reckoned by the inspector; but such permission shall not be given by the inspector if the absence of the teacher will, in his judgment, be injurious to the interests of the school; nor shall this permission be granted to any master or teacher who fails to report, or who has employed the time heretofore given to him otherwise than in visiting schools, as authorized by this regulation.

(3.) *Visitors' Book.*—The master (or teacher) shall keep the visitors book (which is required by law to be furnished by the trustees), in which shall be entered the dates of visits and names of visitors, with such remarks as they may choose to make. The book is to be handed to the visitors for this purpose.

(4.) *Visitors.*—Each master or trustee shall receive courteously the visitors appointed by law, and afford them every facility for inspecting the books used, and examine into the state of the school; he shall keep the visitors' book accessible, that the visitors may, if t¹ choose, enter remarks in it. The frequency of visits to the sch intelligent persons, animates the pupils, and greatly encourag he faithful teacher.

NOTE.—See clause (3) of section 13 of this chapter.

(5.) *Subscriptions, Collections, Presents, &c.*—No collection shall be taken up, or subscriptions solicited for any purpose, or notice of shows or exhibitions given in any public school, without the consent of the trustees.

NOTE.—No master or teacher shall act as agent for any bookseller or other person, to sell, or in any way promote the sale, for such bookseller or person, of any school library, prize or task book, map, chart, school apparatus, furniture, or stationery; nor receive compensation or equivalent for such sale, or for the promotion of such sale, in any way whatsoever; nor receive presents (unless presented to them on leaving the school), nor award, without the permission of the trustees, medals or other prizes of their own to the pupils under their charge. (School Act, sec. 227.)

(6.) *Teachers' Meetings.*—All masters and teachers in cities, towns and villages, shall regularly attend the teachers' meetings, at such times, and under such regulations, as the inspector shall direct, and by study, recitations, and general exercises, strive to systematize and perfect the modes of discipline and teaching in the public schools.

11.—Decisions of the Superior Courts in regard to Teachers.

(1.) *Signing an agreement with a Teacher is a mere approval of the appointment.*— The Court of Queen's Bench has decided that an inspector signing, together with trustees, a contract with a teacher, will be considered as having signed the same only as approving of the appointment, and not as contracting with the teacher.— *Campbell v. Elliott et al, County Model School, Middlesex.* 3 Q. B. R. 167.

(2.) *Trustees agreeing to furnish a Teacher with Fuel must be applied to for it.*— The Court of Queen's Bench has decided that when a teacher charged the trustees upon a special agreement stated to have been made by them, to furnish the said teacher with fuel when required, they could not be charged with a breach of covenant, as a request, with time and place, had not been stated in the teacher's declaration.—*Anderson v. Vansittart et al.* 5 Q. B. R. 335. *Quære* by the Court, whether such an agreement could be enforced?

(3.) *Trustee cannot be sued for Money due.*—The Court of Queen's Bench has decided that trustees refusing to give an order to a teacher for the school fund, according to their agreement with him, cannot be sued for money due, but for the refusal to give the order.—*Quin v. Trustees, 4, Seymour.* 7 Q. B. R. 130.

(4.) *No Rate can be imposed for the payment of an Unqualified Teacher.*—The Court of Queen's Bench has decided that no rate can legally be imposed by trustees for the salary of an unqualified teacher.—*Chief Superintendent of Education, appellant, in re Stark v. Montague et al.* 14 Q. B. R. 473.

(5.) *Trustee and Teacher are not Master and Servant.*—The Court of Queen's Bench has decided that the Master and Servant Act (10 and 11 Vic., c. 23,) does not apply to school trustees and school teachers. Where a school trustee, therefore, has been convicted under it as a master, the conviction was quashed.—*In re Laurence Joice, No.—, Pittsburg, convicted by Robert Anglin, J. P.* 19 Q. B. R. 197.

(6.) *Representation as to the Character of a Teacher by a Ratepayer is a Privileged Communication.*—The Court of Queen's Bench has decided that a representation by the assessed inhabitants of a school section as to the character of a teacher, made with a view of obtaining redress, is a privileged communication, which it is of importance to the public to protect; and such a statement would not be the less privileged if made by mistake to the wrong quarter. Where the libel complained of is clearly a privileged communication, the inference of malice cannot be raised up on the face of the libel itself, as in other cases it might be, but the plaintiff must give extrinsic evidence of actual express malice; he must also prove the statement to be false as well as malicious; and the defendant may still make out a good defence by proving that he had good ground to believe the statement true, and acted honestly under that persuasion. *Quære* by the Court, whether a communition of this nature, made by an inhabitant of any other part of the Province, would not be privileged.—*McIntyre* v. *McBean et al.* 13 Q. B. R. 534.

12.—Miscellaneous Duties of the Public School Teacher.*

(1.) *To hold Public Quarterly Examinations.*—The teacher is required by law "to have at the end of every quarter, a public examination of his school, of which he shall give due notice to the trustees of the school; to any school visitors who reside adjacent to the school, and through the pupils to their parents and guardians."† (Consolidated School Act of 1877, sec. 163, cl. 7.)

(2.) To give the trustees and visitors access at all times, when desired by them, to the registers and visitors' book appertaining to the school.—(*Ibid.* cl. 5.)

(3.) To deliver up any school registers, visitors' books, or school house key, or other school property in his possession, on the demand or order of the majority of the trustee corporation employing him. (*Ibid.* cl. 6.)

NOTE.—"In case of his wilfully refusing to do so, he shall be deemed guilty of a misdemeanor, and shall not be deemed a qualified teacher until restitution be made, and shall also forfeit any claim which he may have against the said trustees." (*Ibid.* cl. 6, (a.)

(4.) *To furnish Information to the Minister, or Inspector.*—"To furnish to the Minister of Education, or to the School Inspector, in the trustees' report or otherwise, any information which it may be in his power to give, respecting anything connected with the operations of his school, or in anywise affecting its interests or character." (Consolidated Act of 1877, sec. 163, cl. 8.)

NOTE.—This duty involves the preparation of reports and returns, as provided in clause (6), section 10 of this chapter, and section 21 of chapter ii.

---

* As to the control of the teacher over the school house, see decision No. 6, of the Court of Queen's Bench, on page 69.

† It will be seen by this clause of the Act, in connection with the first part of the ninety-second section, that "it shall ['shall' here is imperative] be the duty of every teacher of a school : (6) To have at the end of *each quarter* a public examination of his school." Teachers cannot, therefore, lawfully omit this part of their duty.

Form of Teacher's Circular Notice of the Quarterly Examination of his School.

School House of Section No. —,

————————, 187 .

SIR,—As required by law, the quarterly examination of my school will be held on ————day, the — of ————, when the pupils of the school will be publicly examined in the several subjects which they have been taught during the quarter now closing. The exercises will commence at 9 o'clock, a.m., and you are respectfully requested to attend them.

I am, Sir, your obedient servant,

A. B., *Teacher.*

To C. D., School Trustee, (or Visitor).

REMARKS.—A copy of the above notice ought to be sent to each of the trustees, and to as many visitors of the school as possible. The teacher should address a circular notice to those of them who reside within three miles of his school. He is also required to give notice, through his pupils, to their parents and guardians and to the neighbourhood, of the examination. For holidays and vacations, see "General Regulations" in chapter xiv.

13.—Claim of Teacher for Salary until he is paid.*

" Any teacher shall be entitled to be paid at the rate mentioned in his agreement with the trustees (see section 4 of this chapter), even after the expiration of the period of his agreement, until the trustees pay him the whole of his salary, as teacher of the school, according to their engagement with him; and including allowance for holidays and other times, as provided" by the following section, School Act. (*Ibid.* sec. 164.)

NOTE.—This section shall only apply where the teacher prosecutes his claim for salary within three months after it is due and payable by the   `tees. (*Ibid.* cl. (a.)

14.—Teacher entitled to be paid for Holidays, &c.

"Every master or teacher of a public or high school or collegiate institute shall be entitled to be paid his salary for the authorized holidays occurring during the period of his engagement with the trustees, and also for the vacations which follow immediately on the expiration of the school term during which he has served, or the term of his agreement with such trustees." (High School Act, sec. 50.)

NOTE.—Under this provision of the Act, a teacher, whose term of service ends just at the beginning of the Christmas holidays, is entitled to be paid up to the 6th of January. Should the term of service end on the 15th of July, the teacher is entitled to be paid his salary up to the 15th of August.

"In case of sickness, certified by a medical man, he shall be entitled to his salary during such sickness for a period at the rate of not exceeding four weeks for th · entire year; which period may be increased at the pleasure of the trustees." (*Ibid.* sec. 51.)

15.—Matters of difference in regard to Salary.

"All matters of difference between trustees and teachers, in regard to salary or other remuneration, shall be brought and decided in the Division Court by the Judge of the county court in each county." (Public School Act, sec. 165.)

NOTE.—By section 4 of this chapter, it will be seen that no agreement between trustees and teachers, is lawful or binding on the school corporation, unless it is in writing and sealed with the trustees' corporate seal. None other can, therefore, be enforced in a court of law against the corporation. (See decisions of the superior courts, in section 12 of this chapter; see section 14, also.)

---

* The Assessment Law does not exempt a school teacher either from the payment of a tax upon his salary (if over $400 per annum), or from the performance of two days of statute labour, if his salary be under $400.

CHAPTER X.

SUPERANNUATION OF TEACHERS AND INSPECTORS.

1.—Persons entitled to Retiring Allowance.

1. Every male teacher of a public or separate school holding a certificate of qualification.

2. Every female public or separate school teacher holding a like certificate.

3. Every legally qualified master or teacher of a high school or collegiate institute.

4. Every public or high school inspector.

2.—Preliminary Conditions on which the right to the Retiring Allowance depends.

1. Each person must have contributed to the superannuation fund the sum of four dollars per annum, in half-yearly payments, during and for the period of his or her teaching school (public, separate, or high), or in respect of his or her receiving aid from said fund.

2. Where such subscription is not paid within the year, the amount to be contributed for each such year is five dollars.

3. In cases where the applicant has been teaching prior to the year 1854, the applicant shall contribute at the rate of four dollars per annum for such years; the subscriptions for these years will be deducted from the retiring allowance payable for the first year.

4. Where the applicant has not taught in any year prior to 1854, he is to remit only for the years since that period during which he has actually taught school.

5. Back subscriptions or arrears, as above, are to be remitted before the applicant, if a teacher, has ceased to teach.

6. The teaching may either be in a public, separate or high school; and in the case of public or high school inspectors, the period during which the inspector is entitled to receive his allowance may be computed both in respect of the time during which he has actually taught school, or has been engaged in inspecting.

7. Every male teacher of a public or separate school is required to pay into the fund at least four dollars annually in half-yearly sums; while every female teacher of a public or separate school, master or teacher of a high school, or public or high school inspector, may pay this at their option while engaged in teaching or inspecting (as the case may be).

8. In the case of the high school master, or public or high school inspector, the sum of four dollars per annum only is required to be paid by them in respect of subscriptions and arrears for the years previous to the year 1874; but any arrears for that or subsequent years shall be *pro rata* at the rate of five dollars per annum.

9. Persons who are now inspectors are entitled to be allowed for years during which they were acting as township or county local superintendents under the former School Law.

3.—Subsequent Conditions to be complied with before Payment of Annual Retiring Allowance is granted.

1. Every teacher or inspector who complies with the foregoing preliminary conditions as to contribution to the fund is absolutely entitled, on reaching the full age of sixty years, to retire from the teaching profession at his discretion, and to receive an allowance at the rate of six dollars per annum for every year of teaching service in this Province.

The Education Department must, however, be furnished with satisfactory evidence of such teacher possessing a good moral character, as to his or her age, and the length of service as a teacher or inspector (as the case may be).

2. Every teacher or inspector who is under sixty years of age, having contributed as aforesaid, and is disabled from practising his profession, is entitled to the like allowance on furnishing the like evidence, and upon also furnishing the Department, from time to time, with satisfactory evidence of his being so disabled.

3. The teacher who holds a first or second class provincial certificate, or is a head master of a high school or collegiate institute, or a public or high school inspector, is entitled to receive the further allowance at the rate of one dollar per annum for every year of service while holding such certificate, and teaching or acting as head master under it, or of service as a public or high school inspector (as the case may be).

4. The retiring allowance ceases to be payable at the close of the year of the death of the recipient.

5. In the case of applicants who have reached the full age of sixty years, the particulars contained in the form numbered 1 must be furnished to the Department, with such proof as the Minister may require.

6. In the case of any applicant under sixty years of age, on the ground that he or she is disabled from practising his or her profession, the particulars contained in form number 2 must be furnished, together with evidence thereof to the satisfaction of the Minister; and in all applications of this nature, the applicant is required to submit himself or herself for examination touching his or her disability before such one or more registered medical practitioners as the Minister may appoint; and the applicant will not be entitled to any retiring allowance unless the Minister, upon such examination, is satisfied that such disability exists.

7. Any retiring allowance is liable to be withdrawn in any year unless the disability continues; and the recipient is annually to present himself to the inspector in order that he may report thereon to the Minister.

4.—Subsequent Conditions on which Allowances will cease to be made.

1. In case the teacher or inspector fails to maintain a good moral character, which is to be vouched for, when required, to the satisfaction of the Department.

2. In case the disability of any recipient under sixty years of age has ceased to exist upon evidence satisfactory to the Department.

3. In case the teacher, with the consent of the Department, resumes the profession of teaching, or inspecting, payment of his allowance is to be suspended during such period, and until he shall be again placed on the superannuation list; any additional period of teaching shall be allowed for on compliance with the prescribed conditions.

5.—Provision in cases of Withdrawal or Decease.

1. Any teacher or inspector who is not entitled to an allowance from the fund, on retiring from the service, shall receive back one-half of all sums contributed by him or her.

2. Any teacher who has retired from the profession, and received back one-half the amount paid in by him or her to the fund, and who subsequently resumes the practice of teaching, shall thereupon forthwith pay, through the inspector of the city or county, to the Education Department, the sum so refunded to him.

3. In case of the decease of any teacher or inspector, without having been placed on this fund, his or her wife or husband, as the case may be, or other legal representative, shall be entitled to receive back all sums paid in to the fund by such teacher, with interest at the rate of seven per cent. per annum.

4. In any case where the claim of an applicant for a retiring allowance is refused on the ground of non-compliance with the prescribed conditions, then such applicant shall be entitled to receive back one-half of the sums contributed by him or her to the fund.

5. In cases where the contribution to the fund commenced before the year 1871, then the amount to be returned shall be the full amount so paid in by every such teacher, but without interest.

6. Any municipal council, public or high school board, or board of education may, in its discretion, supplement out of local funds the amount of any pension payable by the Department from this fund.

7. The municipal treasurer or other treasurer of school moneys, is required at the end of each half-year to pay over to the order of the inspector, the amount of money in such treasurer's hands, which represents the deductions from salaries of male teachers to this fund for each half-year, or which is otherwise payable by any male teacher to the fund, and the inspector is required to deduct from his cheque, or order, in favour of any male teacher, the sum of two dollars for each half-year in respect of each school.

CHAPTER XI.

RELATION OF INSPECTORS TO PUBLIC SCHOOL TEACHERS.

[NOTE.—No public school inspector shall, during his incumbency, hold the office of trustee of a high or public school, nor act as head master of a high school, or master or teacher of a public school.]

1.—Oversight of Public Schools by an Inspector.

The School Law requires each inspector of public schools "to see that all the schools are managed and conducted according to law." It also declares that he "shall have the oversight of all public schools in the townships and villages within the county or union of counties, or part of the county or union of counties, for which he shall be appointed," and shall "have all the powers in each municipality within his jurisdiction, and be subject to all the obligations conferred or imposed on inspectors by law, according to such instructions as may be given to him, from time to time, by the Hon. the Minister of Education." (Sec. 194, cls. 1 and 2.)

2.—Inspector's Visitation of Schools.

The law requires every county inspector "to visit every public school within his jurisdiction twice a year, unless oftener required to do so by the county council which appointed him, or for the adjustment of disputes, or otherwise." (Sec. 194, cl. 3.)

NOTE.—The regulations require the inspector to devote, on an average, half a day to the examination of the classes and pupils in each school, and to record the result of such examination in a book to be kept for that purpose. He shall also make inquiry and examination, in such manner as he shall think proper, into all matters affecting the condition and operations of the school, the results of which he shall record in a book, and transmit it, or a copy thereof, annually, on completing his second half-yearly inspection, to the Education Department; (but he shall not give any previous notice to the teacher or trustees of his visit.) (See Regulations.)

3.—Authority of an Inspector in a School.

The authority of an inspector in a school, while visiting it, is supreme; the master, teachers, and pupils are subject to his direction; and he shall examine the classes and pupils, and direct the masters or teachers to examine them, or to proceed with the usual exercises of the school, as he may think proper, in order that he may judge of the mode of teaching, management, and discipline in the school, as well as of the progress and attainments of the pupils. (*Ibid.*)

4.—Inspector's Procedure in the Visitation of Schools.

On entering a school, with a view to its inspection, and having courteously introduced himself to the teacher (if a stranger), or, if otherwise, having suitably addressed him, the inspector shall:

(1.) Note in the inspector's book the time of his entrance, and on leaving, the time of departure from the school.

(2.) See whether the business going on, corresponds with that assigned to that particular hour on the time-table, and generally whether the arrangements which it indicates agree with the prescribed programme of studies, and are really carried out in practice. If not, he should at once privately notify the teacher of the omission, and the penalty for neglect to observe the regulations.

(3.) Examine the general and daily registers, and other school records, and take notes of the attendance of pupils, number of classes in the school at the time of his visit, &c.

(4.) Observe the mode of teaching, the management of the school, and generally its tone and spirit: also, whether the bearing, manner, and language of the teacher, his command over the pupils, and their deportment at the time of his visit are satisfactory. (*Ibid.*)

5.—Intercourse with Teachers and Pupils.

In his intercourse with masters and teachers, and during his visit to their schools, the inspector should treat them with kindness and respect, counselling them privately on whatever he may deem defective or faulty in their manner and teaching; but by no means should he address them authoritatively, or in a fault-finding spirit, in presence or hearing of the pupils. (*Ibid.*)

6.—See to Attendance of Children at School.

The inspector should see that the provisions of the School Act, in regard to the rights of every child in the municipality under his jurisdiction, to attend some school, are not allowed to remain a dead letter.

NOTE.—The inspector should also see that the trustees take the yearly school census of the section, and, in cases of delinquent parents, charge the school fee or report the cases to the magistrate, as required by the School Act.

7.—Teachers Visiting other Schools.

County and city inspectors shall have authority to allow teachers to visit schools, under the restrictions contained in clause (2), section 11 of chapter ix.

8.—Payments to Teachers' Superannuation Fund.

The law requires each inspector of public schools to deduct two dollars semi-annually, for the superannuated teachers' fund, from each half-yearly payment made by him on behalf of any male teacher holding a certificate of qualification under his jurisdiction, and transmit the same to the Education Department. (School Act, sec. 194, cl. 16.)

NOTE.—In doing so, the inspector will have to see that the sum of two dollars is deducted from each male teacher's half-yearly salary, whether paid direct to the teacher by the trustees, or by their order on the inspector. (See note to sec. 22, chapter ii, page 24.)

NOTE.—Where trustees pay to a male teacher his whole salary, without accounting to the inspector for the half-yearly payment to the superannuation fund, the inspector should notify the trustees that until the money is sent to him by their treasurer, as required by law, no further apportionment will be paid to their school. This would effectually prevent the evasion sometimes practised in this matter. (See note to next section.)

9.—Cheques to Teachers payable to Themselves.

Any cheques for school money due a section must be made payable to the (qualified) teacher, assistant, or monitor, or his order, and to no other person; and no cheque shall be given to such teacher except on an order signed by a majority of the trustees of the school section, and attested by a lawful corporate seal, and then only for the time during which the teacher has held a legal certificate of qualification, not cancelled, suspended, recalled, or expired. (See note to sec. 22, of chapter ii, page 24.)

NOTE.—In giving cheques to a section in payment for the time during which the school was taught by a male teacher, the half-yearly payment of two dollars to the superannuated teachers' fund must be deducted. In case trustees should pay the outgoing male teacher out of the funds of the section, and then give an order to their next teacher (male or female) for the full amount apportioned to their section, the inspector, being responsible for the money payable to the fund by the outgoing male teacher, must deduct the $2 already due, besides taking the remedial steps indicated in the note to the preceding section. A form of order, which the trustees should send to the inspector, will be furnished by Messrs. Copp, Clark & Co., Toronto, free of postage, for 5 cents. (See note to section 22 of chapter ii, page 24.)

10.—Granting Special Certificates.

The School Law authorizes every inspector "to give to any candidate, *on due examination,* according to the programme authorized for the due examination of teachers, a certificate of qualification to teach school within the limits of the charge of such inspector, until (but no longer than) the next ensuing meeting of the board of examiners of which such inspector is a member." (School Act, sec. 194, cl. 22.)

NOTE.—No such certificate shall be given a second time, or be valid if given a second time, to the same person in the same county." (*Ibid.* sec. 194, cl. 22 (*a.*)

NOTE.—In giving effect to this provision of the Act, inspectors will observe : (1) that they are required to examine all candidates desiring special certificates ; (2) that they are not authorized to grant "permits" without examination ; (3) that the special certificates given can only have the value of those of the third class, and be valid only "within the limits of the charge of the inspector ;" (4) that under no circumstances can they give a special certificate to a teacher who has already previously received one from any (local superintendent or) inspector in the same county; and (5) that no certificate can be given to a teacher who has been rejected by the board of examiners, unless by consent of such board, and under the authority of the Education Department. Inspectors can endorse as valid in their county, third-class certificates given in another county. They can also give certificates to assistants and monitors for a year. (See sec. 14 of this chapter.)

11.—Suspension of Public School Teachers' Certificates.

When an inspector finds it necessary to suspend the certificate of a master or teacher, he should not do so on the mere report of improper conduct, immorality or incompetency, but he should give the master or teacher due notice of the charge against him, and afford him a full opportunity for defence, he should also examine carefully into the alleged facts of the case, and, if necessary, visit the school and assure himself personally of their truth, on the oath or affirmation of witnesses, before proceeding to suspension.

NOTE.—Officers, required by law to exercise their judgments, are not answerable for mistakes in law, or mere errors of judgment, without any fraud or malice.

12.—Inspector to Verify Attendance of Pupils.

The inspector should see that the aggregate attendance of each school is correctly added up, and divided by the divisor for the half year, and that no lost time is made up by teaching on Saturdays, or other holidays, or vacations. (See chapter xiv.) Under clause (2) of section 11 of chapter ix, teachers may, with the consent of the inspector, employ certain days in the year in visiting other schools. In order that the school may not lose a corresponding proportion of the school fund, the inspector is authorized to add a proportionate amount of average attendance for time so employed, or use a smaller divisor.

NOTE.—After having examined and tested the correctness of the return, the inspector should file away and carefully preserve it, so that it may be handed over, with other school documents, to his successor, when he retires from office.

13.—Check against Incorrect Returns.

The half-yearly return of the pupils' names, and number of days in which they attended during each month, will be a check against false or exaggerated returns; as the inspector can, in his visit to any school, take the return with him, compare it with the school register, and make any further inquiries he may deem necessary. He should, also, at his visits to the school, take notes in his book of the school attendance, &c.

NOTE.—The returns, carefully compiled, will furnish materials for the statistical tables in the inspector's report, and will show at what periods of the year the attendance of pupils at the schools is the largest, and how many attend school during two, four, six, &c., months of the year.

CHAPTER XII.

SCHOOLS IN UNORGANIZED TOWNSHIPS.

1.—Formation of School Sections in Unorganized Townships.

In unorganized townships in any county or district it shall be lawful for the stipendiary magistrate thereof and the public school inspector (if any) of the county or district, or for the stipendiary magistrate alone if there be no inspector, and for the inspector alone if there be no stipendiary magistrate, to form a portion of a township, or of two or more adjoining townships, into a school section.

(a) No such section shall, in length or breadth, exceed five miles in a straight line.

(b) Subject to this restriction, the boundaries may be altered by the same authority from time to time, and the alteration shall, go into operation on the twenty-fifth day of December next after such alteration.

(c) No such school section shall be formed except on the petition of five heads of families resident therein. (School Act, sec. 26.) .

2.—Election of Trustees in Unorganized Townships.

After the formation of such a school section, it shall be lawful for any two of the petitioners, by notice posted for at least six days in not less than three of the most public places in the section, to appoint a time and place for a meeting for the election, as provided by law, of three school trustees for the section. (*Ibid.* sec. 27.)

NOTE.—The elections of trustees under this section are to be conducted as pointed out in chapter vi. of these Lectures.

3.—Powers of Trustees in Unorganized Townships.

The trustees elected at such meetings, or at any subsequent school meetings of the section, as provided by law, shall have all the powers and be subject to all the obligations of public school trustees generally. (*Ibid.* sec. 28.)

NOTE.—The powers and duties of trustees are fully explained in chapter ii.

4.—School Assessment Roll in Unorganized Townships.

The trustees so elected shall annually appoint a duly qualified person to make out an assessment roll for the section, and shall transmit a certified copy thereof to the stipendiary magistrate (or inspector.)

(a) It shall be the duty of the stipendiary magistrate, or of the inspector if there be no stipendiary magistrate, to examine the said roll, and correct any errors or improper entries which he shall perceive therein. (*Ibid.* sec. 29.)

NOTE.—For explanation in regard to assessment roll, see chapter iii.

5.—Revision of the School Assessment Roll.

A copy of the said roll, as so corrected, shall be open to inspection by all persons interested, at some convenient place in the section, notice whereof, signed by the stipendiary magistrate, or inspector, if there be no stipendiary magistrate, is to be annually posted in at least three of the most public places in the section, and shall state the place and the time at which the magistrate or inspector will hear appeals against said assessment roll.

. (a) Such notice shall be posted as aforesaid by the trustees for at least three weeks prior to the time appointed for hearing the appeals. (*Ibid.* sec. 30.)

6.—School Assessment Roll Appeals.

All appeals are to be made in the same manner and after the same notice, as nearly as may be, as appeals are made to a court of revision in the case of ordinary municipal assessments, and the magistrate (or inspector) shall have the same powers as such court of revision. (*Ibid.* sec. 31.)

7.—Power of Magistrate or Inspector in Appeal Cases.

(1.) The magistrate or inspector has power "to try all complaints in regard to persons wrongfully placed upon or omitted from the roll, or assessed at too high or too low a sum." (Assess. Act, Rev. Stat. ch. 180, sec. 53.)

(2.) *Oaths to Parties.*—The magistrate, or inspector, may, at his discretion, administer an oath to any party or witness before taking his evidence,. The oath may, however, be required by the opposite party. (*Ibid.* sec. 54.)

(3.) *Summons of Witnesses.*—The magistrate, or inspector, may issue a summons to any witness, to attend at the confirmation of the roll, but he need not attend unless he be tendered fifty cents a day. After such tender should he "fail without good and sufficient reason, to attend, he shall incur a penalty of $20, to be recoverable with costs by and to the use of any person suing for the same." (Amended Assess. Act, sec. 55.)

(4.) *Assessment on Real Property.*—In regard to real property, the magistrate, or inspector, "after hearing upon oath the complainant," and the party who assessed the property, "and any witness adduced, and, if deemed desirable, the party complained against, shall determine the matter, and confirm or amend the roll accordingly." (Assess. Act, sec. 56, cl. 15.)

(5.) *Assessment on Personal Property.*—If the party assessed complains of an overcharge on his personal property, or taxable income, he, or his agent, may make a declaration of the true value of personal property, without deducting ordinary debts (though debts on the property itself are to be stated), and of gross income from all sources; and no abatement shall be made from the amount of income in respect to debts, except debts due for or on account of such personal property; and the magistrate or inspector, shall, thereupon, enter the person assessed at such an amount of personal property, or taxable income, as is specified in such declaration, unless he shall be dissatisfied with the declaration; in which case the parties concerned, may be examined on oath as to "the correctness of the declaration," and the magistrate, or inspector "shall confirm, alter or amend the roll, as the evidence shall seem to warrant." (*Ibid.* sec. 56, cl. 14.)

(6.) *Failure of Parties to Appear.*—"If either party fails to appear, either in person, or by an agent, the magistrate, or inspector, may proceed *ex parte.*" (*Ibid.* sec. 56, cl. 17.)

(7.) *Roll Confirmed and Signed.*—On the final confirmation of the roll by the magistrate, or inspector, it is to be signed as passed, and handed to the trustees for their guidance.

8.—Confirmed School Assessment Roll Binding.

The annual roll, as finally passed and signed by the magistrate (or inspector), shall be binding upon the trustees and ratepayers of the section until the annual roll for the succeeding year is passed and signed, as aforesaid. (School Act, sec. 32.)

9.—Certificates to Teachers in New Districts.

Any public school inspector may,' under such general regulations or instructions as may be prescribed according to law, examine and give special certificates, from time to time, to teachers in new and remote townships in the county, riding or division in which he is inspector; which certificates shall be valid in such townships for the periods mentioned in the regulations. (*Ibid.* sec. 194, cl. 24.)

CHAPTER XIII.

GENERAL PROVISIONS OF THE LAW & REGULATIONS APPLICABLE TO ALL SCHOOLS.

1.—All Public Schools shall be Free Schools.

All " public schools shall be free schools, and the trustees of school sections, and the municipal councils of cities, towns, villages and townships shall, in the manner now provided by law, levy and collect the rate upon the taxable property of the school division or municipality (as the case may be),' to defray the expenses of such schools, as determined by the trustees thereof." (Public School Act, sec. :7.)

Note.—The manner of raising funds by rural school trustees is pointed out in chapters ii. and iii. of these Lectures.

2.—Residents in one Section sending to another Section.

" Any person residing in one school section, division, city, town or village, and sending a child or children to the school of a neighbouring school section, division, city, town or village, shall, nevertheless, be liable for the payment of all rates assessed on his property for school purposes in the section, division, city, town or village in which he resides, as if he sent his child or children to the school of such section; and such child or children shall not be returned as attending any other than the school of the section in which the parents or guardians of such child or children reside." (*Ibid.* sec. 160.)

Note.—For full explanation of the law relating to non-residents, see chapter iv. of these Lectures.

3.—Exception as to Separate Schools and Non-residents.

The law declares that the foregoing section "shall not apply to persons sending children to or supporting separate schools; or prevent any person who may be taxed for public school purposes on property situate in a different school section from that in which he resides, from sending his children to the school of the section in which such property may be situate, on as favourable terms as if he resided in such section." (*Ibid.* section 160; see chapter iv. of these Lectures.)

NOTE.—School fees or rate bills can now be charged to non-residents, who have the right to send their children to the school nearest to them,—to the support of which they are not ratepayers. (See, however, chapter iv.)

4.—Foreign Books not to be used without permission.

"No person shall use any foreign books in the English branches of education, in any model or public school, without the express permission of the Department of Education; and no portion of the legislative school grant shall be applied in aid of any public [or separate] school in which any book is used that has been disapproved by the Department of Education, and public notice given of such disapproval." (*Ibid.* sec. 11.)

5.—Pupils not to be required to join in Religious Exercises.

"No person shall require any pupil in any such school to read or study in or from any religious book, or to join in any exercise of devotion or religion objected to by his or her parents or guardians; but within this limitation, pupils shall be allowed to receive such religious instruction as their parents and guardians desire, according to any religious regulations provided for the government of public schools." (*Ibid.* sec. 9.)

NOTE.—The teacher of each public school is requested to hear the pupils of the school repeat the Ten Commandments once a week. (See next section.)

6.—Opening and Closing Exercises of each Day.

1. As Christianity is the basis of our whole system of elementary education, that principle should pervade it throughout. The section (144) quoted above, secures individual rights, as well as recognizes Christianity.

2. In the section of the Act thus quoted, the principle of religious instruction in the schools is recognized, the restrictions with which it is to be given are stated, and the exclusive right of each parent and guardian on the subject is secured.

3. The public school being a *day*, and not a *boarding school*, rules arising from domestic relations and duties are not required; and as the pupils are under the care of their parents and guardians on Sabbaths, no regulations are called for in respect to their attendance at public worship.

4. With a view to secure the Divine blessing, and to impress upon the pupils the importance of religious duties, and their entire dependence on their Maker, the Council of Public Instruction recommends that the daily exercises of each public school be opened and closed by reading a portion of Scripture, and by prayer. The Lord's Prayer alone, or the forms of prayer hereto annexed, may be used, or any other prayer preferred by the trustees and master of each school.

5. The Lord's Prayer shall form part of the opening exercise, and the Ten Commandments be taught to all the pupils, and be repeated at least once a week. But no pupil should be compelled to be present at these exercises against the wish of his parent or guardian, expressed in writing to the master of the school. (Public School Regulations, chapter i.)

NOTE.—The forms of prayer provided for in these regulations will be found on page 2 of the cover of the daily school register.

7.—Weekly Instruction by the various Clergy.

In order to correct misapprehension, and define more clearly the rights and duties of trustees and other parties in regard to religious instruction in connection with the public schools, it is decided by the Council of Public Instruction that the clergy of any persuasion, or their authorized representatives, shall have the right to give religious instruction to the pupils of their own church, in each school house, at least once a week, after the hour of *four* o'clock in the afternoon; and if the clergy of more than one persuasion apply to give religious instruction in the same school house, the trustees shall decide on what day of the week the school house shall be at the disposal of the clergyman of each persuasion at the time above stated. But it shall be lawful for the trustees and clergyman of any denomination to agree upon any hour of the day at which a clergyman, or his authorized representative, may give religious instruction to the pupils of his own church, provided it be not during the regular. hours of the school. (*Ibid.*)

8.—No School Official shall act as Book Agent.

"No teacher, trustee, inspector, or other person officially connected with the Education Department, the normal, model, public or high schools or collegiate institutes, shall become or act as agent for any person or persons to sell, or in any way to promote the sale for such person or persons, of any school library, prize or text book, map, chart, school apparatus, furniture or stationery or to receive compensation or other remuneration or equivalent for such sale, or for the promotion of sale in any way whatsoever." (School Act, sec. 227.)

9.—Legal Definition of the Public "School Fund."

"The legislative school grant, together with at least an equal sum raised annually by local assessment, shall constitute and be called the

6

public school fund of such county, township, city, town or village."
(*Ibid.* sec. 139.)

10.—Restriction as to the Application of the "School Fund."

"No part of the salaries of the Minister of Education, school inspectors, nor of any other persons (except teachers employed), or of any expenses incurred in the execution of this Act, shall be paid out of the said public school fund, but such fund shall wholly and without diminution be expended in the payment of teachers' salaries." (*Ibid.* sec. 213.)

11.—Conditions of paying the School Fund to Schools.

"No cheque shall be given for any portion of the school fund to any school section which has not been conducted according to law, and to the regulations provided under its authority." (*Ibid.* sec. 194, cl. 14.)

It will thus be seen that the county inspector has no option but to withhold the school fund apportioned to a section, in consequence of the neglect or refusal of the trustees to comply with the law itself, or with the regulations framed under its authority, especially as these regulations have, by the statute, the force of law. This neglect or refusal applies to the school house, site and premises, school accommodation, supply of maps and apparatus, employment of the necessary number of qualified teachers and assistants, and also to all of those matters which are designed to promote the efficiency of the school and the success of the teachers employed.

12.—Penalty for Disturbing Public Schools.

"Any person who wilfully disturbs, interrupts, or disquiets the proceedings of any school meeting authorized to be held by this Act, or any one who interrupts or disquiets any public school established and conducted under its authority, by rude or indecent behaviour or by making a noise either within the place where such school is kept or held, so near thereto as to disturb the order or exercises of the school, shall, for each offence, on conviction thereof before a justice of the peace, on the affidavit of one credible witness, forfeit and pay for public school purposes to the school section, city, town or village within which the offence was committed, such sum not exceeding twenty dollars, together with the costs of conviction, as the said justice may think fit; or the offender may be indicted and punished for any of the offences hereinbefore mentioned as a misdemeanor." (*Ibid.* sec. 249.)

13.—Miscellaneous Decisions of the Superior Courts.

(1) *Embezzlement—A Trustee, not being Secretary-Treasurer, cannot receive or retain school moneys.*—The Court of Common Pleas has decided that a school

trustee having money in his hands, not as secretary and treasurer of a board, or in any official capacity, cannot embezzle such money, his duty as trustee not requiring or authorizing him to receive it.—*Farris v. Irwin*, No. 16 Darlington, 10 C. P. R. 116.

(2.) *Loan to School Trustees—Personal liability—Change of School Site.*—Two of the trustees of a school section, wishing to change the school site, called a meeting of the freeholders and householders, who rejected the proposal. The two trustees thereupon chose an arbitrator, assuming to act under sec. 30 Consol. Stat. U. C. ch. 64, but none was chosen by the freeholders and householders, and under the advice of the Deputy Superintendent the trustees called another meeting, at which a motion to appoint such arbitrator was rejected. The trustees' arbitrator and the local superintendent thereupon made an award changing the site. A special meeting was then called to consider how the money should be raised to carry out the change, at which the conduct of the trustees and the change was strongly disapproved of. The two trustees thereupon petitioned the township council, stating that the ratepayers were desirous of purchasing a new site, and asking for a loan of $400, "for which the trustees will bind themselves to pay the interest annually, and the principal when due." This was granted, and secured by two instalments, as follows :—

"We, the undersigned, Trustees of School Section No. 11, do hereby promise to pay the Treasurer of the Corporation of Toronto Township, or," &c.
            (Signed)   M. }
                                         D. } *Trustees.*

with the corporate seal affixed. The money was expended for the purpose mentioned. The township corporation having sued the trustees individually on these notes, and on the common counts : *Held*, that they could not recover on the notes, for, (1) They were payable to the treasurer ; and (2) The defendants were not personally liable upon them. *Held*, also, *Wilson, J.* dissenting, the defendants were not liable upon the common counts either, for the intention of all parties plainly was that the trustees as a corporation should be bound, not the defendants personally ; and there being no fraud and concealment on their part, the fact that they as a corporation had no authority to borrow, nor the plaintiffs to lend, could not, under the circumstances, make them personally liable. *Semble, per Richards, C. J.*, that under section 30, the difference of opinion as to the change of site authorized a reference to arbitration ; but that the refusal of the freeholders and householders to name an arbitrator did not enable the other two arbitrators to proceed, the proper course being to compel the appointment by mandamus. *Per Wilson, J.*, the difference of opinion must be as to the position of the new site, after the change has been agreed to by the ratepayers, not as to whether there shall be a change ; and the arbitration, therefore, was unauthorized.—*The Corporation of the Township of Toronto v. McBride et al., Executors of William McBride*, 29 Q. B. R. 13.

CHAPTER XIV.

REGULATIONS RESPECTING CERTIFICATES OF QUALIFICATION TO TEACH IN THE PUBLIC SCHOOLS.

1.—Third-Class Certificates.

I. The conditions upon which county boards are authorized to grant third-class certificates are as follows:

1. In order to be qualified to receive a third-class certificate, the candidate must be, if a male, eighteen years of age; if a female, seventeen.

2. The candidate must have passed the prescribed examination in literary and scientific subjects.

3. Any person who shall pass the intermediate examination, or the prescribed examination in literature and science for second or first-class certificates, shall be deemed to have passed the examination in literature and science prescribed for third-class certificates.

4. The candidate must subsequently have attended, for one session, at a county model school, and must have obtained from the head master of such school, and from any examiners whom the Minister may appoint, a certificate of his fitness to teach.

5. He must produce evidence that he is of good moral character.

II. The duration and renewals of third-class certificates are governed by the following provisions:—

1. A third-class certificate shall be valid only in the county where given, and for three years only.

2. No candidate shall be permitted to enter a second time for a third-class certificate, except by special permission of the Minister, on the recommendation of the county inspector.

3. As cases may arise where third-class teachers are unable to qualify themselves for passing the examination prescribed for second-class certificates; and as, nevertheless, it is desirable, in some such cases, that the teachers who are in this position should not be excluded from the profession; the Minister may, on the recommendation of the county inspector, allow a third-class teacher, of experience and proved ability as a teacher, to teach permanently, or for any specified length of time, on a third-class certificate within the county for which the certificate has been granted. But each such case must be specially reported on by the inspector, who shall state fully the grounds which, in his opinion, warrant the departure from the ordinary rule.

2.—Second-Class Certificates.

I. The conditions upon which second-class certificates are to be granted are as follows:

1. In order to be qualified to receive a second-class certificate, the candidate must have passed the examination in literature and science prescribed for second-class certificates.

2. In the event of the intermediate examination being so modified as to be, in the judgment of the Minister, a full equivalent for the examination in literature and science for second-class certificates, any candidate passing the intermediate shall be held to have passed the examination in literature and science for second-class certificates, grade B. Any candidate passing the prescribed examination in literature and science for first-class certificates shall be held to have passed the examination in literature and science for second-class certificates.

3. The candidate must have taught, successfully, for at least one year, in a public or separate school in the Province of Ontario, and must have attended, for one session, in a provincial normal school, and must have obtained from the principal of such school, and from the examiners, a certificate of his fitness to teach on a second-class certificate.

4. He must produce evidence that he is of good moral character.

3.—First-Class Certificates.

I. The conditions upon which first-class certificates are to be granted are as follows:—

1. In order to be qualified to receive a first-class certificate, the candidate must have passed the prescribed examination in literary and scientific subjects.

2. He must also have attended for one year at a provincial normal school, after obtaining a second-class certificate, and have received from the principal of such school, and from such examiners as the Minister may appoint, a certificate of his fitness to teach on a first-class certificate, or otherwise he must have taught successfully for two years on a second-class certificate, and have passed such examination as the Minister may prescribe, to test his fitness to teach on a first-class certificate.

3. He must produce evidence that he is of good moral character.

4.—General.

1. The examinations in literature and science prescribed for first and second-class certificates respectively, may be passed at any time; but no certificate of any class will be granted till all the conditions above indicated have been satisfied.

NOTE.—Teachers holding first or second-class certificates, granted anywhere in the British Dominions, may be admitted to examination for first and second-class certificates respectively, in this province, provided that they produce satisfactory evidence of good moral character and time of actual experience, as required of other teachers.

Graduates in arts who have proceeded regularly to their degrees in any university in the British Dominions, and who produce satisfactory evidence of having taught successfully for one year, and satisfactory proof of good moral character, may be admitted to the examination for first-class certificates without previously obtaining third and second-class certificates.

EXAMINATION OF CANDIDATES.

I.—NON-PROFESSIONAL EXAMINATION.

By the non-professional examination of public school teachers is meant the examination which candidates for the several classes of certificates must pass in literature and science, according to the scheme hereinafter laid down ; which examination must be passed, in the case of candidates for third-class certificates, before they are admitted to the county model schools, and, in the case of candidates for second-class certificates, before they are admitted to any of the normal schools.

1.—Time and Place of Examination.

1. The examinations of all candidates for first and third-class certificates shall be held in the month of July, in each year, on the days appointed by the Minister.

2. The examinations of candidates for second-class certificates shall be held twice a year, concurrently with the intermediate examinations in July and December.

3. Candidates for first-class certificates shall be examined at Toronto and Ottawa ; candidates for second and third-class certificates, at the county towns.   If there is no county town in any inspectoral division in which an examination is held, the candidates shall be examined at such place as may be appointed by the inspector.

4. Candidates for first-class certificates, and pupils of the normal schools shall be examined at the normal schools ; the examinations of all other candidates shall be held in such building or buildings as may in each case be appointed by the inspector.

5. The inspector shall give at least three weeks' public notice of the time and place of each examination, in such manner as he shall deem expedient.

2.—Notice to be given by Intending Candidates—Testimonials—Identification.

1. Every person who proposes to present himself at any examination, shall send in to the presiding inspector, not later than the 1st of June, and, in the case of second-class certificates, the 10th of November also, preceding each examination, a notice stating the class of certificate for which he is a candidate, and the description of certificate he already possesses, if any; such notice to be accompanied by the testimonials required by the regulations.

2. Each candidate shall satisfy the presiding examiner as to his personal identity before the commencement of the second day's examination. Instances of personation of candidates having occurred, the examiners are expected to use all necessary vigilance in this respect.

3. Any person detected in attempting to personate a candidate is to be reported to the Department, and he will thereupon be deprived of his certificate and standing as a teacher.

3.—Mode of Conducting Examinations.

1. Every presiding inspector shall send to the Education Department, one month before the time of the examination, a list of the names of those who intend to present themselves for second-class certificates. To each name so sent the Department will affix a *number*, which must be employed by the candidate instead of his usual signature throughout the entire examination.

2. Candidates for first-class certificates shall notify the Department, at least five weeks before the examination, as to the place at which they intend to present themselves for examination, and shall at the same time forward the testimonials required by the regulations.

3. The Department will provide envelopes of convenient dimensions, to be sent out with the first and second-class examination papers—one envelope with each paper.

4. The county public school inspector shall preside, and be responsible for the proper conduct of the examinations, and for the safe-keeping, unopened, of the examination papers until the time of examination; but in case of any inability to attend, he shall send to the Education Department, for the approval of the Minister, or Deputy, one month before the examination, the name of the person whom he intends to appoint his substitute at those examinations at which he himself cannot preside, otherwise the Department will make the appointment.

5. When more than one room is required for the candidates, an inspector's substitute must be appointed for each room, to preside in his stead.

6. The presiding inspector shall transmit to the Education Department, on the first day of the examination, a copy of the following declaration, signed by himself and the other examiners (but such declaration shall not be required more than once from any examiner):

"I solemnly declare that I will perform my duty of examiner without fear, favour, affection or partiality towards any candidate."

7. The presiding examiner shall subject the candidates for third-class certificates to *viva voce* examinations in reading, of the result of which a record shall be made and reported to the Department.

4.—Directions for Presiding Examiners.

1. Places shall be allotted to the candidates for second-class certificates, so that they may be at least five feet apart. All diagrams or maps having reference to the subjects of examination shall be removed from the room. Candidates for third-class certificates must be placed sufficiently far apart to prevent copying.

2. All these arrangements shall be completed, and the necessary stationery shall be distributed and placed in order on the desks of the candidates at least *fifteen* minutes before the time appointed for the commencement of the examination.

3. No candidate shall be allowed to leave the room within one hour after the issue of the examination papers in any subject; and if he then leave he shall not be permitted to return during the examination in the subject then in hand.

4. Punctually at the time appointed for the commencement of the examination in each subject, the presiding examiner shall, in the examination room, and in the presence of the candidates, break the seal of the envelope containing the examination papers, and give them at once to the candidates. The papers of only one subject shall be opened at one time.

5. The inspector shall further see that at least one examiner is present during the whole time of the examination, in each room occupied by the candidates. (1) He shall, if desirable, appoint one or more of his co-examiners to preside at the examination in any of the subjects named in the programme. (2) If intermediate and second-class candidates are being examined together, the following rule applies:—No trustee, master or teacher of the school concerned can be appointed to preside, and no master or teacher of the school shall be present during the examination, in the room with the candidates.

6. Punctually at the expiration of the time allowed, the examiner shall direct the candidates to stop writing, and cause them to hand in their answer papers immediately, those for first and second-class being duly fastened in the envelopes.

7. The inspector, at the close of the examination on the last day, shall secure in a separate parcel the fastened envelopes of each candidate for a second-class certificate, and on the same day shall forward by express (prepaid), to the Education Office, the package containing all the parcels thus separately secured, together with all certificates of character, ability, and experience in teaching, which such candidate may have presented to the board, and the schedule in the form provided. The inspector shall, at the same time, sign and forward a solemn declaration (according to a form provided by the Department), that the examinations have been held and conducted in strict conformity with the regulations, and fairly and properly in every respect; and also, with the papers of each candidate, a certificate to the Department, that he has been satisfied as to the personal identity of such candidate, upon proper grounds.

8. In the case of candidates for third-class certificates, he shall see that the written answers are without delay read and reported on by the county board, and he shall thereupon see that these answers, and all reports thereon, as approved by the board, together with the list of certificates issued by it, are also, as soon as possible after the close of the examinations, transmitted by express (prepaid) to the Education Department.

9. When two or more rooms are occupied by candidates for second-class certificates, the examiner, in his report to the Department, shall indicate the candidates who were placed in the several rooms respectively.

10. In examining the answers of third-class candidates, two examiners at least should look over and report on each paper.

11. The Central Committee of Examiners shall assign numerical values to each question, or part of a question, on the examination papers for third-class certificates, according to their judgment of its relative importance. The local examiners shall give marks for the answers, according to the value assigned to each question and the completeness and accuracy of the answer.

12. In order to obtain a third-class certificate, the marks must not be less than one-half of the aggregate value of all the papers for certificates of that rank.

13. Should any candidate be detected in copying from another, or allowing another to copy from him, or in taking into the room any books, notes, or anything from which he might derive assistance in the examination, or in talking or whispering, it shall be the duty of the presiding examiner, if he obtain clear evidence of the fact at the time of its occurrence, to cause such candidate at once to leave the room; neither shall such candidate be permitted to enter during the

remaining part of the examination, and his name shall be struck off the list. If, however, the evidence be not clear at the time, or be obtained after the conclusion of the examination, the examiner shall report the case, if that of a third-class candidate, at a general meeting of the examiners, who shall reject the candidate if they deem the evidence conclusive. If the case be that of a first or second-class candidate, it shall be reported to the Department.

14. The inspector shall furnish to the Education Department full returns and all necessary information in matters relating to the results of the examinations. Any points relative to the examination for third-class certificates, on which a majority of the examiners do not agree, shall be referred to the Education Department for decision.

5.—Rules to be Observed by Candidates.

1. Candidates shall be in their allotted places before the hour appointed for the commencement of the examination. If a candidate be not present till after the appointed time, he cannot be allowed any additional time. No candidate shall be permitted, on any pretence whatever, to enter the room after the expiration of an hour from the commencement of the examination. When the order to stop writing is given, every candidate shall obey it immediately.

2. Every candidate shall conduct himself in strict accordance with the regulations, and should he give or receive any aid, or extraneous assistance of any kind in answering the examination questions, he will be liable not only to the loss of the whole examination, but to the forfeiture or withdrawal of his certificate, at any time afterward when the discovery is made that such aid or assistance has been given or received.

3. Candidates shall observe the regulation respecting copying, &c., in clause 13, preceding section.

4. Every candidate for a first or second-class certificate shall write his NUMBER (not his name) very distinctly at the top of each page of his answer papers in the middle; and is warned that for every page not bearing his number he is liable to receive no credit from the examiners.

5. If a candidate for a first or second-class certificate write his name or initials, or any distinguishing sign or mark on his paper other than the number assigned him by the Department, his paper will be cancelled.

6. Candidates for first or second-class certificates, in preparing their answers, shall write on one side only of each sheet, placing the number of each page at the top, in the right hand corner. Having written the distinguishing NUMBER on each page, and having arranged the

answer papers in the order of the questions, they shall fold them once across, place them in the envelopes accompanying the question papers, and write on the outside of the envelopes the distinguishing numbers and the subjects of examination. They shall then securely fasten the envelopes and hand them to the presiding examiner.

7. Candidates for third-class certificates, in preparing their answers, shall write on one side only of each sheet, and having arranged their papers in the order of the questions, shall fold them once across and write on the outside sheet their names, the name of the examining county board, the date and the subject of the paper. After the papers are handed in, the examiners shall not allow any alterations thereof, and the presiding inspector shall be responsible for the subsequent safe-keeping of the same, until he has transmitted them, with all surplus examination papers, to the Education Department.

6.—Candidates from the Normal Schools.

1. Such of the foregoing regulations respecting the examination of candidates generally as are applicable, shall also govern the examination of candidates from the normal schools ; and the principals thereof, respectively, shall send to the Education Department, one month before such examination, a list of the names of the intending candidates for first and second-class certificates, respectively. The Department will affix a number to each name so sent, and this number shall be signed by the candidate, in lieu of his name, to each one of his papers of answers to the questions.

2. The duties of presiding examiner shall be discharged by one of the members of the Central Committee, to be named by the Minister.

3. During the examination and previous week of preparation all the rules and regulations of the normal school shall remain in full force, and any infringement thereof shall be summarily dealt with by the principal.

4. During the time in each day while the examination is actually proceeding, the examiner shall have control and be responsible for maintaining discipline in the examination hall amongst the candidates ; and at all other times and occasions during each day of the examination, the principal's authority shall have full force and effect.

7.—Appeals to the Department.

Any candidate for a third-class certificate shall have the right to appeal to the Education Department against the decision of the local board of examiners. Every such appeal shall be made in writing to the Department within two weeks from the time when the decision is known to the appellant. The appeal must specify the particular objections, and a fee of $2 be deposited with the Department.

8.—Subjects of Examination.

1. For *Third-Class Certificates.*

Reading.—To be able to read any passage selected from the authorized reading-books intelligently, expressively, and with correct pronunciation.

Spelling.—To be able to write correctly any passage that may be dictated from the reading-book.

Etymology.—To know the prefixes and affixes and principal roots.

Grammar and Composition.—Grammatical forms and definitions. Analysis and parsing of prose and easy verse. Changing the construction of sentences. Short narratives or descriptions. Rendering of poetry into prose. Familiar and business letters.

N.B.—In regard to teachers in French or German settlements, a knowledge of the French or German grammar respectively may be substituted for a knowledge of the English grammar, and the certificates to the teachers expressly limited accordingly. The county councils, within whose jurisdiction there are French or German settlements, are authorized to appoint one or more persons (who in their judgment may be competent) to examine candidates in the French or German language.

English Literature.—To be able to answer easy questions on works or portions of works to be prescribed from time to time.

History.—The leading events of English and Canadian history.

Geography.—The maps of the continents, Canada, Ontario, Great Britain and Ireland, and the principal dependencies of the empire. Map drawing. Rudiments of physical, mathematical and political geography.

Arithmetic.—Simple and compound rules. Reduction. Vulgar and decimal fractions. Proportion. Interest, discount, stocks, exchange. Square root.

Algebra.—The elementary rules and easy simple equations.

Euclid.—Definitions, postulates and axioms. Book I.

To be able to write legibly and neatly.

2. For Second-Class Certificates.

Spelling.—To be able to write correctly a passage dictated from any English author, and to spell all non-technical English words.

Etymology.—To know the prefixes, affixes, and principal Latin and Greek roots. To be able to analyze etymologically words selected from reading-books.

Grammar.—To be thoroughly acquainted with the definitions and grammatical forms and rules of syntax, and to be able to analyze and parse, with application of said rules, any sentence in prose or verse.

N.B.—In the case of teachers in French or German settlements, the intermediate papers in French or German respectively may be substituted for the paper in English grammar, and the certificates to the teachers expressly limited accordingly.

Composition.—The framing of sentences. Familiar and business letters. Rendering of poetry and prose themes.

English Literature.—Critical reading of works or portions of works to be prescribed from time to time by the Department.

History.—To have a good knowledge of general English and Canadian history. Outlines of general European history.

Geography.—To have a fair knowledge of political, physical, and mathematical geography. Map geography generally; Canada and the British Empire more particularly.

Arithmetic and Mensuration.—To be thoroughly familiar with arithmetic in theory and practice, and to be able to work problems in the various rules. Areas of rectilinear figures, and volumes of right parallelopipeds and prisms. The circle, sphere, cylinder and cone.

Algebra.—Elementary rules; factoring; greatest common measure; least common multiple; square root; fractions; surds; simple equations of one, two, and three unknown quantities : easy quadratics.

Euclid.—Books I., II., with problems.

Natural Philosophy.—To be acquainted with the properties of matter and with the elementary principles of statics, hydrostatics, and pneumatics.

Chemistry.—Combustion. The structure and properties of flame. Nature and composition of ordinary fuel.—The atmosphere. Its constitution. Effects of animal and vegetable life on its composition.—Water. Chemical peculiarities of natural waters, such as rain water, river water, spring water, sea water.—Hydrogen, oxygen, nitrogen, carbon, chlorine, sulphur, phosphorus, and the more important compounds.—Combining proportions by weight and by volume. Symbols and nomenclature.

Writing.—To be able to write legibly and neatly.

Book-keeping.—To understand book-keeping by single and double entry.

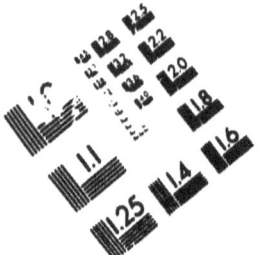

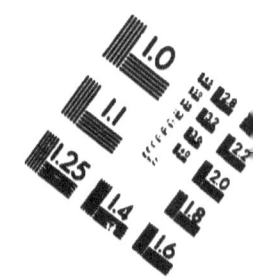

**IMAGE EVALUATION
TEST TARGET (MT-3)**

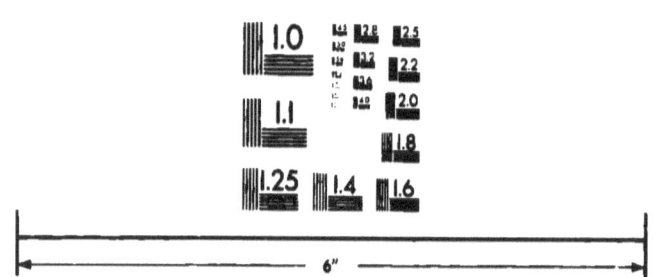

6"

Photographic
Sciences
Corporation

23 WEST MAIN STREET
WEBSTER, N.Y. 14580
(716) 872-4503

3. For First-Class Certificates.

Reading.—To be able to read intelligently and expressively a passage selected from any English author.

Spelling.—To be able to write correctly a passage dictated from any English author, and to spell all non-technical English words.

Etymology.—The same as for second-class certificates.

Grammar.—To be thoroughly acquainted with the subject.

Composition.—The same as for second-class certificates.

English Literature.—To have a general acquaintance with English literature and its history, and a fuller knowledge of special eras and authors to be from time to time prescribed by the Department.

History.—A special knowledge of certain periods, to be prescribed from time to time by the Department.

Geography.—Physical geography. Ancient geography, as far as is necessary for understanding the history of Greece and Rome. A special knowledge of the geography of the British Empire.

Arithmetic and Mensuration.—To know the subject in theory and practice. To be able to solve problems with accuracy, neatness and despatch. To be ready and accurate in solving problems in mental arithmetic. To be familiar with rules for mensuration of surfaces and solids.

Algebra.—The same as for second-class certificates, with quadratic equations, proportion, progressions, permutations and combinations, and the binomial theorem.

Euclid.—Books I., II., III., IV. Definitions of V. and Book VI., with exercises.

NOTE.—For female teachers, the first three books only of Euclid are required. If, however, the candidate desires a certificate of eligibility as an examiner, the same examination must be passed in Euclid as is required of male teachers.

Natural Philosophy and Physical Science.—The properties of matter. The elementary principles of statics, hydrostatics, pneumatics and dynamics. A good general acquaintance with the subjects of heat, light and electricity.

Chemistry.—The chief physical and chemical characters, the preparation, and the characteristic tests of oxygen, hydrogen, carbon nitrogen, chlorine, bromine, iodine, fluorine, sulphur, phosphorus and silicon. Carbonic acid, carbonic oxide, oxides and acids of nitrogen, ammonia, olefiant gas, marsh gas, sulphurous and sulphuric acids, sulphuretted hydrogen, hydrochloric acid, phosphoric acid, phosphuretted hydrogen, silica. Combining proportions by weight and by volume; general nature of acids, bases and salts; symbols and nomenclature. The atmosphere—its constitution, effects of animal and vegetable life upon its composition; combustion; structure and properties of flame; nature and composition of ordinary fuel. Water —chemical peculiarities of natural waters, such as rain water, river water, spring water, sea water.

Botany.—Applications of chemistry to agriculture, an introductory course of vegetable anatomy and physiology, illustrated by the examination of at least one plant in each of the crowfoot, cress, pea, rose, parsley, sunflower, mint, nettle, willow, arum, orchis, lily and grass families; systematic botany; flowering plants of Canada.

Physiology.—General view of the structure and functions of the human body; the vascular system of the circulation; the blood and the lymph; respiration; the function of alimentation; motion and locomotion; touch, taste, smell, hearing and sight; the nervous system.

Book-keeping.—The same as for second-class certificates.

II.—PROFESSIONAL EXAMINATION.

1.—County Model Schools.

1. A candidate for a third-class certificate shall, at the close of his term of attendance at a county model school, be examined in the work of the term, together with any other subjects connected with the practice of teaching, which the Minister may appoint.

2. Before being admitted to this, which may be called his professional examination, the candidate must receive a certificate from the head master of the model school that he has, throughout the term, paid satisfactory attention to his duties, and that he is, in the opinion of the head master, a fit person to be allowed to go up to the examination.

3. The professional examinations in the county model schools shall be held on such days as the Minister may appoint, and shall be conducted by the several county boards.

4. They shall be partly oral and partly in writing, according to a scheme to be prepared by the Central Committee, and to be approved by the Minister.

2.—Normal Schools.

Candidates for Second-Class Certificates.

1. A candidate for a second-class certificate shall, at the close of his term of attendance at the normal school, be examined in the work of the term, together with any other subjects connected with the practice of teaching, which the Minister may appoint.

2. Before being admitted to this, which may be called his professional examination, the candidate must receive a certificate from the principal of the normal school that he has, throughout the term, paid satisfactory attention to his duties, and that he is, in the opinion of the principal, a fit person to be allowed to go up to the examination.

3. The professional examinations of the normal school students shall be partly oral and partly in writing; they shall be held at the several normal school seats, on such days as the Minister may appoint, and shall be conducted by the Central Committee.

Candidates for First-Class Certificates.

1. A candidate for a first-class certificate, being a student of the normal school, shall, at the close of his session of attendance at the normal school, be examined in the work of the session, together with any other subjects connected with the practice of teaching, which the Minister may appoint.

2. Before being admitted to this examination, the candidate must receive a certificate from the principal of the normal school that he has, throughout the session, paid satisfactory attention to his duties, and that he is, in the opinion of the principal, a fit person to be allowed to go up to the examination.

3. The examination shall be partly oral and partly in writing; they shall be held at the several normal school seats on such days as the Minister may appoint, and shall be conducted by the Central Committee.

4. Candidates for first-class certificates who are not normal school students, shall undergo their professional as well as their non-professional examination at one of the normal school seats, at the same time and on the same papers with those candidates for first-class certificates who are normal school students.

3.—Qualifications of Monitors and Assistants—Their Certificates.

Inspectors can (under the following regulations) grant certificates of qualification, which shall be valid for one year, to any senior pupil or other person, to act as assistant teacher or monitor, in a public school. The regulations are as follows:—

At the request in writing of any public or separate school corporation, a public school inspector may admit to examination any senior pupil, or other candidate for the position of monitor or assistant in such public or separate school, on the following conditions:

(a) The pupil or other candidate shall present to the inspector a certificate of good moral character, signed by a clergyman.

(b) The subjects of examination for the position of monitor shall be reading, writing, spelling, and the elementary parts of grammar, geography and arithmetic.

(c) The subjects of examination for the position of assistant teacher, shall be those prescribed for third-class certificates.

N.B.—A competent knowledge of those subjects at the discretion of the inspector shall be required.

(d) No candidate shall be admitted to examination for a monitor's certificate under fifteen years of age, or from a lower class than the fourth; nor for a certificate as an assistant under sixteen years of age, nor from a lower class than the fifth.

(e) No certificate shall be given for a longer period than one year. Such certificate may be specially renewed for twelve months at the discretion of the inspector; but no certificate shall be granted a third time without re-examination.

(f) A certificate may be suspended or cancelled at the discretion of an inspector, for any cause which he may deem sufficient to warrant it.

(g) All certificates granted, suspended, or cancelled, and all other information desired, shall be duly reported by the inspectors to the Minister.   (Revised School Act, sec. 194, cl. 25, and Official Regulations.)

N.B.—When the pupils enrolled in a public school amount to more than fifty, and less than one hundred, the trustees must employ an assistant teacher.

NOTE.—Under no circumstances can an assistant or monitor holding certificates from an inspector under these regulations, be placed in charge of a school.   (See section 12 of chapter xliii.)

4.—Certificates to Teachers in remote Townships.

Inspectors are also authorized (under the prescribed regulations) to grant certificates of qualification to teachers, which shall be valid for a stated period, in new and remote townships.   (Sec. 194, cl. 24.)

CHAPTER XV

TERMS, HOURS OF DAILY TEACHING, HOLIDAYS AND VACATIONS.*

1. *Terms and Vacations.*—The public school year shall consist o. two terms: the first shall begin on the third day of January, and end on the seventh day of July; the second shall begin on the eighteenth day of August, and end on the twenty-third day of December. There shall be two vacations during the year for public schools; the summer vacation shall be from the eighth day of Jui to the seventeenth day of August inclusive; the winter vacation from the twenty-fourth day of December to the second day of January inclusive; in the case of united public and high schools, and also of public schools in cities, towns, and incorporated villages, in which high schools are situate, the vacations shall be the same as are prescribed for high schools.*

The high schools shall open on the seventh day of January, and close on the Thursday before Easter; they shall reopen on the first Tuesday after Easter, and close on the thirteenth day of July; they shall reopen on the first day of September, and close on a twenty-second day of December. There shall be three vacations for high schools in the year: the Easter vacation to extend from Good Friday to Easter Monday, inclusive; the summer vacation shall begin on the fourteenth day of July, and end on the thirty-first day of August; and the Christmas vacation shall begin on the twenty-third day of December, and close on the sixth day of January; and the high school boards are authorized to dismiss during the period when the intermediate examination is going on in such schools, those pupils who are not engaged in the examination.

2. *Holidays.*—The schools shall be taught on all week days during the term except Saturdays, the anniversary of the birth of the Sovereign, Dominion Day, any local municipal holiday, and such day as may be appointed by the Governor, or other competent authority, for a public fast or thanksgiving throughout the Province.

---

* In order also to enable the Education Department to make an equitable proportionment to Roman Catholic separate schools in cities, towns and villages where united high and public schools exist, it is required that both the public and separate schools shall observe the regulations affecting holidays and vacations in the high schools; in ascertaining the average yearly attendance at the separate schools, the inspector will report to the Department for its consideration such days on which, under the discipline of the Roman Catholic Church, the school is closed, and mention what, if any, equivalents in time have been made up on other days in which the public schools are closed.

3. *Hours.*—The exercises of the day shall commence not later than NINE o'clock a.m., and shall not exceed six hours in duration, exclusive of the time allowed at noon for recreation, and of not less than ten minutes during each forenoon and each afternoon. Nevertheless, a less number of hours of daily teaching may be determined upon in any school at the option of the trustees. All teachers shall be in their respective schools, and open their rooms for the reception of pupils, at least fifteen minutes in the morning and five minutes in the afternoon, before the specified time for beginning school; and during school hours they shall faithfully devote themselves to the duties of their office. Care must be taken to have the school house ready for the reception of pupils at least *fifteen* minutes before the time prescribed for opening the school, in order to afford shelter to those who may arrive before the appointed hour.

NOTE.—No lost time can be lawfully made up by any teacher on any holiday or during the vacations; and if so made up, it must be disallowed by the inspector.

5. *All Agreements* between trustees, masters and teachers shall be subject to the foregoing regulations; and no master or teacher shall be deprived of any part of his salary on account of observing allowed holidays and vacations, and masters and teachers shall be entitled to salary for the holidays or vacations immediately following the close of their period of service.

6. *Absence—Sickness.*—No master or teacher shall be absent from the school in which he or she may be employed without permission of the trustees or inspector, except in case of occasional sickness, in which case the absence of such teacher shall be immediately reported to the trustees; and no deduction from the salary of a teacher shall be made on account of such sickness, as certified by a medical man, at the rate of not exceeding four weeks for the entire year; which period may be increased at the pleasure of the trustees.

7. *Visiting Schools.*—The inspector may permit a public school master, or teacher, to be absent two of the ordinary teaching days in each half year, for the purpose of visiting and observing the methods of classification, teaching and discipline practised in other schools than that in which he or she teaches; and such visit, with the name of the school or schools visited, shall be duly reported by such master or teacher to the inspector. Each public school master and teacher must give at least three days' notice to the trustees. In order that no loss of apportionment may accrue to any school in consequence of the master's absence under this regulation, a proportionate amount of average attendance will be credited to the school for the time so employed by the teacher; but under no circumstances can lost time be lawfully made up by teaching on any of the prescribed holidays or half holidays, nor will such time be reckoned by the Department,

or be allowed by the inspector. Such permission shall not be given by the inspector if the absence of the teacher will be, in his judgment, injurious to the interests of the school; nor shall this permission be granted to any master or teacher who fails to report, or who has employed the time heretofore given to him otherwise than in visiting schools, as authorized by this regulation.

The privilege of visiting other schools for two days each half year is also permitted to the head master of a high school, but it is necessary that he should give three days' notice to the trustees, and also obtain the consent of the Education Department, in order that he may not be absent at the inspector's visit. He should note his time of absence on the half-yearly return, in order that the proportion of attendance may be credited and the school saved from loss.

CHAPTER XVI.

DUTIES OF PUPILS IN THE PUBLIC SCHOOLS.

1. *Cleanliness and Good Conduct.*—Pupils must come to school clean and neat in their persons and clothes. They must avoid idleness, profanity, falsehood, and deceit, quarrelling and fighting, cruelty to dumb animals; be kind and courteous to each other, obedient to their instructors, diligent in their studies, and conform to the rules of their school.

2. *Tardiness* on the part of pupils shall be considered a violation of the rules of the school, and shall subject the delinquents to such penalty as the nature of the case may require, at the discretion of the master.

3. *Leaving before Closing.*—No pupil shall be allowed to depart before the hour appointed for closing school, except in case of sickness, or some pressing emergency; and then the master's or teacher's consent must first be obtained.

4. *Absence.*—A pupil absenting himself from school, except on account of sickness, or other urgent reasons satisfactory to the master, forfeits his standing in the class, and his right to attend the school for the remainder of the quarter.

5. *Excuses.*—Any pupil not appearing at the regular hour of commencing any class of the school which he may be attending, without a written excuse from his parent or guardian, may be denied admittance to such school for the day, or half day, at the discretion of the teacher.

6. *Punctual Attendance.*—Every pupil, once admitted to school, and duly registered, shall attend at the commencement of each term, and continue' in punctual attendance until its close, or until he is regularly withdrawn by notice to the teachers to that effect; and no pupil violating this rule shall be entitled to continue in such school, or be admitted to any other, until such violation is certified by the parents or guardians to have been necessary and unavoidable, which shall be done personally or in writing.

7. *What School to Attend.*—Pupils in cities, towns, and villages shall be required to attend any particular school which may be designated for them by the inspector, with the consent of the trustees. And the inspector alone, under the same authority, shall have the power to make transfers of pupils from one school to another.

8. *Absence from Examination.*—Any pupil absenting himself from examination, or any portion thereof, without permission of the master, shall not thereafter be admitted to any public school, except by authority of the inspector, in writing; and the names of all such absentees shall be reported by the master immediately to the trustees; and this rule shall be read to the school just before the examination days, at the close of each quarter.

9. *Going to and from School.*—Pupils shall be responsible to the master for any misconduct on the school premises, or in going to or returning from school, except when accompanied by their parents or guardians, or some person appointed by them, or on their behalf.

10. *Supply of Books.*—No pupil shall be allowed to remain in the school unless he is furnished with the books and requisites required to be used by him in the school; but in case of a pupil being in danger of losing the advantages of the school, by reason of his inability to obtain the necessary books or requisites, through the poverty of his parent or guardian, the trustees have power to procure and supply such pupil with the books and requisites needed.

11. *Fees for Books.*—The fees for books and stationery, &c., as fixed by the trustees in cities and towns, whether monthly or quarterly, or fees for non-resident pupils, shall be payable in advance; and no pupil shall have right to enter or continue in the school until he shall have paid the appointed fee, or it shall have been paid on his behalf.

12. *Property Injured.*—Any property of the schools that may be injured or destroyed by pupils, must be made good forthwith by the parents or guardians, under a penalty of the suspension of the delinquent pupil. (See (7) of regulation 3 of the "*Powers and Duties of Masters.*")

13. *Contagious Diseases.*—No pupil shall be admitted to, or continue in, any of the public schools who has not been vaccinated, or who is afflicted with, or has been exposed to, any contagious disease, until all danger of contagion from such pupil, or from the disease or exposure, shall have passed away, as certified in writing by a medical man.

14. *Effects of Expulsion.*—No pupil shall be admitted to any public school who has been expelled from any school, unless by the written authority of the inspector. (See regulation 4, *Duties of Masters*.)

15. *Certificate on Leaving.*—Every pupil entitled thereto shall, when he leaves, or removes from a school, receive a certificate of good conduct and standing, in the form prescribed, if deserving of it.

CHAPTER XVII.

REVISED REGULATIONS AS TO SCHOOL ACCOMMODATION.

I.—RURAL SCHOOLS.

The public school law as now amended (see sec. 102, cl. 8) requires trustees of rural school sections to provide adequate school accommodation in their sections, "so as to accommodate at least two-thirds of the children who have the right to attend the school of the section, according to the census taken by the trustees for the next preceding year." This includes all children resident in the school section between the ages of 5 and 21 years, and also children from adjacent school sections, whom the trustees are required to admit upon certain conditions.

The school accommodation required by the Act for school houses hereafter to be erected, is hereby defined as follows, and these requisites are to be construed to apply also to existing school houses, so far as the circumstances of each section may enable them to be complied with, without pressing unduly upon the resources of the section. Inspectors will see to the carrying out of the regulations. Special cases of omission or difficulty to be reported to the Department for decision or advice.

1.—Rural School Site, House and Appendages.

1. *50 Children and under—Site.*—When the number of children resident in a section is fifty or under, the site for the school house shall not be less than half an acre in extent.

2. *Over 50 Children—Site.*—When the number exceeds fifty, the site shall not be less than an acre in extent.

3. *Kind of House.*—On such site there shall be a substantial school house of wood, brick, stone, etc. (the kind to be determined at the pleasure of the trustees), set back at least ten yards from the road or street; the walls of the house shall not be less than ten feet high in the clear. It shall not contain less than twelve square feet on the floor for each child who has the right to attend (to the extent of two-thirds of the total number as aforesaid), so as to allow an area in each room, or gallery, for at least one hundred and twenty cubic feet of air for each child, including space for teacher, platform, and passages between the seats.* It shall also be sufficiently warmed and ventilated, and the premises properly drained, to the satisfaction of the inspector.

4. *Separate Entrances.*—In school houses for more than fifty pupils, there shall be separate entrances for boys and girls, with necessary cap and cloak rooms attached.

5. *Fences.*—The school premises shall be strongly fenced, the play yards in the rear of the school house being invariably separated by a high and tight board fence, or wall; the front ground being planted with shade trees.

6. *Well.*—A well, or other means of procuring water for the school, satisfactory to the inspector.

7. *Offices.*—Proper and separate offices for both sexes shall be provided at some little distance from the school house, and suitably enclosed or otherwise masked.

2.—School House Accommodation and Teachers.

3. *50 Resident Children.*—For a school section having fifty resident children or under, there shall be a house with school room and comfortable sittings for the children, and the trustees may also provide a gallery or class room. There shall be one teacher and, at the option of the trustees, a monitor to aid the teacher.

4. *100 Resident Children.*—For a section having one hundred resident children, there shall be a house with two class rooms with comfortable sittings (one for an elementary and one for an advanced division), and the trustees are recommended to provide a gallery. There shall be a teacher and assistant, and at the option of the trustees, a monitor.

---

* Thus, for instance, a room for fifty children would require space for 6,000 cubic feet of air. This would be equal to a cube of the following or equivalent dimensions in feet, viz.: 30 × 20 × 10, which is equivalent to a room 30 feet long by 20 wide, and 10 feet high.

NOTE.—*Temperature.*—In winter, the temperature during the first school hour in the forenoon or afternoon, should not exceed 70, and 60 degrees during the rest of the day.

5. *150 Resident Children.*—For a section having one hundred and fifty resident children, a house having one gallery and two good class rooms with comfortable sittings, and one teacher, an assistant and monitor; or a house having a gallery and two apartments (one for an elementary and one for an advanced department), with a teacher and two assistants. If one commodious building cannot be secured, two houses may be provided in different parts of the section, with a teacher and assistant in each. A monitor may be appointed to prepare the younger children for the master, the duty of the assistant being confined to the preparation of the more advanced pupils.

6. *Over 150 Resident Children.*—For a section having over one hundred to one hundred and fifty resident children, the regulation for accommodation for village schools shall apply.

II.—Cities, Towns and Villages.

It is the duty of the public school board, under the amended law of 1877, to determine the number and kinds of schools to be established and maintained in the municipality; and in order that this duty may be definitely regulated, the following are to be observed by the respective public school boards, that is to say:—

1.—School House Accommodation and Teachers.

1. *150 to 200 Resident Children.*—For a village or town school, having from one hundred and fifty to two hundred resident children, a brick, stone or frame house shall be provided by the board, having in it one or two galleries, and three apartments (one for an elementary, one for an intermediate division, and one for the highest division), and by means of a sliding door, one good class room, at least, common to the two latter; also three teachers and an assistant, and at the option of the trustees, a monitor. The area of each room or gallery shall be such as to secure a space of at least one hundred cubic feet of air to each child to be accommodated therein. If necessary, schools may be provided at the pleasure of the trustees for the different departments in different parts of the village, town or division.

2. *200 Resident Children and upwards.*—For any village or town having two hundred resident children and upwards, a house or houses with sufficient accommodation for the different elementary and advanced divisions shall be provided as above prescribed.

III.—As to all Public Schools.

The Offices shall be constructed so as to possess these essential particulars, viz.:—

1. The privy building, or closet, should be masked from view, and its approaches equally so.

2. There should be little or no exposure to mud or wet weather in reaching it.

3. There should be no unpleasant sight or odour perceptible.

4. The apartment should be well finished.

5. It should be kept entirely free from cuttings, pencillings, or markings, and scrupulously clean.

6. There should be, at least, two privies attached to each mixed school, and they should be so separated that neither in approaching nor occupying them can there be either sight or sound observed, in passing, or from one to the other. This cannot be effected by a mere partition; nothing can secure the object but considerable distance, or extra heavy brick or stone walls resting on the ground. It is a serious error ever to omit this precaution.

Furniture and Apparatus.—Desks, seats, black-boards, maps, library, presses, books, and other furniture necessary for the efficient conduct of the school, shall be furnished.

Suggestions as to School Buildings.

Trustees and school boards are recommended to pay due attention to the following particulars in the erection of school houses, viz.:

1. The school house should be but *one story high*, in rural sections.

2. A separate room should be provided for every fifty pupils enrolled in the school. By means of sliding doors, these separate rooms could be thrown into one on special occasions.

3. Provision should be made for one or more gallery or class rooms in every school, according to its size as heretofore prescribed.

4. Separate entrances with outer porches to the school house or room, for boys and girls, should invariably be provided, where the number of pupils is over fifty.

5. The entrance porches should be external to the school house.

6. The external doors of the school house should open outwards.

7. The school rooms must be well ventilated.

8. The light should be admitted to the school and class room behind or at the left of the children, and either from the east or north; but in no case should the children face it.

9. The window sashes should be made to move up and down on pulleys, and the sills should be about four feet above the floor.

10. Each school house should be provided with a bell.

11. If the house be brick, care should be taken to make the walls hollow, but air-tight, otherwise the walls will be damp inside.

NOTE.—Each inspector is furnished, by the Department, with Dr. Hodgins' book on *School Architecture*, which supplies useful plans and suggestions for the guidance of trustees; and the inspector will assist the trustees in giving effect to the above recommendations.

CHAPTER XVIII.
REGULATIONS RESPECTING "TEACHERS' ASSO-CIATIONS."

The following regulations shall apply to and govern "teachers' associations:"

1. In each county or inspectoral division a teachers' association shall be formed, the object of which shall be to read papers and discuss matters having a practical bearing on the daily work of the school room.

2. *Officers.*—The officers of the association shall be a president, vice-president, and secretary-treasurer. There shall also be a management committee of five. The officers of the association and the management committee shall be elected annually.

3. *Meetings.*—The association shall meet once during each half year, and shall continue in session two days, which shall be deemed as visiting days. The time and place of the first meeting shall be fixed by the inspector. Subsequent meetings shall be held on such days and at such places as the association may determine.

4. *Sessions.*—The sessions on the first day shall be from 9 a.m. to 12 m., and from 2 p.m. to 5 p.m. On the second day from 9 a.m. to 12 m., and from 2 p.m. to 4 p.m.

5. *Programme.*—The subjects for discussion and order of business shall be determined by the management committee and officers of the association; and all teachers in the county or inspectoral division shall be notified of the subjects at least one month before each meeting. The work of the association shall be as practical as possible; and at every meeting illustrative teaching of classes should form a prominent part of the proceedings. All questions and discussions foreign to the teacher's work should be avoided. The programme for the first meeting of the association shall be drawn up by the in-

spector, and by such teachers as he may call to his assistance, of which notice shall be given as above.

6. It is recommended that a public lecture be delivered either by the inspector or some other suitable person on the evening of first day's meeting.

7. In case one or more persons should be appointed by the Department for the purpose of more fully enabling the associations to accomplish the purposes for which they are established, such persons shall report upon the efficiency of each association with the view of its being entitled to receive from the Department and county corporations the appropriations authorized by the legislature, and, in the meantime, such report shall be made by the inspector.

8. In case the inspector, from time to time, reports to the Department the continued efficiency of the association, the association will then, and not otherwise, be entitled to receive the said legislative and county appropriations.